TO WHOM IT MAY CONCERN

J. S. COOPER

Dedicated to my uncle Gordon Albert Case, who passed away on July 9th, 2020, from COVID-19 complications. Thank you for always being a shining light. May your creative genius live on in your son, Jean Louis. I pray your soul rests in peace.

BLURB

To Whom It May Concern,

I would like to request more information about the assistant job I saw advertised in Sunday's newspaper with the high six-figure starting salary. I have a bachelor's degree in English with many years of work experience, and I think I would be a suitable fit for the job. My questions are as follows:

1. What is the exact nature of the job?

2. Is it a strict requirement that I live with the boss? If so, can I have friends and others over?

3. The ad states there is a uniform. May I ask what sort of uniform? And why?

Also, in lieu of sending a photograph, I've sent a picture of my friendly dog that would also join me if I were to get the job.

Yours sincerely,

Savannah Carter

Ms. Carter,

How do you know you'll be a suitable fit for the job if you do not know the nature of the work? My ad specifically stated I am looking for an MBA grad, not an English grad who knows nothing about the actual world.

1. I would discuss this in the interview.

2. Yes, you would live with me. And I allow no guests.

3. The uniform would be provided on your first day. You don't need to know why.

The job advertisement asked for a personal photo; is this your way of telling me you look like a dog?

Today must be your lucky day because you're the only person who responded to my ad. Are you available for a phone interview tomorrow?

The Wade Hart

CHAPTER 1

"Ten billion jobs in New York City, and I'm not qualified for any of them," I grumbled at my best friend, Lucy, and chewed down harder on the black pen in my mouth. "I'm so screwed."

Black ink seeped onto my lower lip and I pulled the pen out of my mouth quickly before I poisoned myself. Which would be just my luck the way my life was going.

"There are loads of jobs you could get, Savannah." Lucy walked over and sat next to me on our old white Ikea couch that looked more yellow than white now that it was five years old. "You have a degree. That alone qualifies you for, like, one billion jobs."

"You would think so, right?" I handed her the newspaper that was in my hands. "I've not seen one ad looking for recent college grads with degrees in English."

Why hadn't anyone told me that getting a degree in English was like flushing $100,000 down the toilet? Well, more like $150,000 by the time I'd finished paying off my student loans. It would have been nice if someone had told me. Maybe I could have taken the money and gone traveling around the world instead. Not that I thought the govern-ment would have loaned me the money for that.

"What about being a teacher?" Lucy said helpfully, a hopeful smile on her face. "You could be an English teacher."

"I would need to have a certificate of accreditation to teach in an elementary or high school." I flopped back in the seat and sighed dramatically, shaking my long brown pony-tail and running my fingers through the tendrils that had escaped at the front. "I have no certificates, and I looked at the test online yesterday and it looked hard as hell."

"What about a nursery school, then?"

"Are you joking?" I raised an eyebrow at her. "I did not go to college for four years to read kids' books to little brats."

"Yeah, well, with that attitude, you wouldn't get the job, anyway." Lucy grinned at me, and I laughed despite myself. "Savannah, you have to be flexible. There are many jobs you can get."

"I don't want to work at McDonald's again." I shuddered at the memory. "I already told you how that went for me before. I lasted three weeks, and I gained fifteen pounds. Fifteen pounds in three weeks. How is that even possible?"

"Well, you're not in high school anymore. You have more self-control. No need to eat all the fries that you can fit in your mouth just because they're free."

"They weren't even free." I sighed. "I had a discount."

"Well, we digress." Lucy looked over the ads in the paper in front of her. "I'm not telling you to go back to fast food, but a paycheck is a paycheck, and you know we've got bills coming up soon." Her voice trailed off as she glanced up at me and chewed her lip nervously. Lucy had been my best friend since we'd met four years ago at a poetry slam contest in Brooklyn. We'd both been new to the city, starting our first year in college and excited to explore the city. She'd been at NYU in Greenwich Village renting a small apartment in

St. Marks Place, and I'd been all the way up in Morningside Heights, near Harlem at Columbia University, sharing a dorm room with a girl from Germany. After the first two years, we'd rented a small one-bedroom in the Upper West Side, with Lucy's dad paying the rent and me paying the bills. It had worked out well, but now that we'd graduated, Lucy's dad had said he would no longer pay the rent, and I couldn't use student loans to pay the bills anymore, so we were up a creek without a paddle. I had three hundred dollars in the bank and needed a job quickly.

"We're screwed," I whined. My scruffy black and grey terrier, Jolene, ran up to me. She jumped on the couch, her big brown eyes staring at my face in concern as she sniffed the air, hoping she'd get lucky and find some random pieces of food. "How are we going to pay the rent?"

I rubbed Jolene between the ears as she snuggled up on my lap and tried to think of a way to come up with $5000 in the next couple of weeks. Not only did I have rent coming up, but my first student loan payment was due and it was more than I'd thought it would be.

"Let's not panic." Lucy's eyes continued scanning the newspaper. "There has to be something you can do." She looked up at me. "You know if I had any extra money, I would totally help you."

"I know." I smiled at her gratefully. Lucy was a generous person, but her internship at a minor publishing house barely paid her enough to cover her half of the rent and bills. She was lucky that she didn't have student loans, or she'd be in just as bad a position as I was. "And thanks for asking your boss if they had another position available for me, but maybe it's for the best that they didn't. Could you imagine us living *and* working together?"

"No." She shook her head vehemently. "I couldn't deal with your mess in the office and at home. Sorry."

"Hey, no fair! It was your turn to do the dishes last night, and they're still in the sink."

"That's because you burned almost every pot we own trying to make that chili dish you read about online." She pursed her lips. "I do not understand how you ruined chili. You know that's a dish you can make in a crockpot."

"Hey, no need to show off just because you nearly got on *Top Chef*."

"As an assistant to one of the producers, not as one of the chefs. My cooking skills are no better than yours." Lucy winked at me. "I just don't lie to myself and pretend I'm a Michelin star chef."

"I don't think I'm a Michelin star chef. I would like to think that I can whip up some excellent food, though."

"You can whip up an awesome grilled cheese." Lucy's face froze, and she turned to me looking excited. "What if you got a job in that grilled cheese restaurant on the Lower East Side?"

"You have got to be joking, right?"

"No, but wait a second. Look at this." She held the newspaper up and grabbed the pink highlighter that was lying on the side of the couch. She circled an ad in the paper and brought it over to me. "This sounds promising."

"What does it say? High-paying job for English grad that loves doing poetry readings at small coffee shops?"

"Hey, I enjoy doing poetry readings as well, and my degree is in filmmaking."

"At least you were smart enough to double major in economics. My dumb ass was too busy reading Shakespeare and Chaucer."

"An old English man would love you. Or maybe a priest."

"Why would a priest love me?"

"The Canterbury Tales was one of your favorites, right? Wasn't that about a pilgrimage?"

"Lucy, sometimes I swear if you weren't my best friend, I would kill you. Me reading a collection of stories written in Middle English doesn't qualify me to work in a church."

"Before you kill me, check out this job. "Wanted: college grad with outstanding personality. High-paying job in sales. No experience necessary. Need people to start now."

"Hmm," I grabbed the newspaper from her. "I am a college grad and I do have an outstanding personality." I beamed my ten-thousand-dollar smile at her and shook my long brown hair with the too expensive honey-blonde high-lights so I could feel it hitting my back. "I don't really know what the job is."

"Sales. It says right there."

"But what am I selling?"

"How am I supposed to know? Call them and ask."

"Yeah, I guess so." I read the ad again, and then my eyes hit another ad a little bit below it. "Listen to this one: Do you want to earn high six-figures? Seeking professional for a unique job. Prefer MBA grad. Applicant would have to live in and wear a uniform. To apply, send resume and photo-graph to ..."

"I saw that, but it seems a bit off. Why do you have to live in and what sort of uniform?"

"Girl, who cares? High six-figures?" My brain was going into overdrive at the thought of making so much money. "I'd be a frigging maid for high six-figures. That means like over a hundred grand or something."

"Yeah, I would even say higher than that. A hundred grand would be low six-figures." Lucy looked thoughtful. "It seems like it would be close to a million dollars."

"Whoa, could you imagine if I made a million dollars?" I chewed on my lower lip. "I could pay off all my debt and we could move to a two-bedroom apartment and then maybe I could take some time off to concentrate on my poetry book."

"Girl, you don't have an MBA and you're not a professional, plus who knows what the job is ..." Lucy made a face as she shook her head. "It sounds super shady. Plus, you would have to live there."

"You mean you wouldn't like this apartment to yourself for a little bit?"

"Not really." She giggled. "Maybe if I had a boyfriend and was looking to get laid. But I have no boyfriend and haven't been laid in ..." She paused. "Well, you know."

"I know, ugh." I leaned back again and tried not to think of our awful dating situation. For two pretty girls in their early twenties, we had terrible luck with men. Neither one of us had had a serious relationship since we'd been in New York, and seeing as we'd both moved to New York right after high school, it was fair to say that neither one of us had ever had a serious relationship. "Do you think we're the only two twenty-two-year-old virgins in New York City?"

"Yes," she answered immediately and emphatically. "And if you didn't hear me the first time, *yes*. Even the Mormon girls on their year off come to the city and get laid."

"How is it even possible we don't have boyfriends?" I threw the newspaper on the couch and stood up. Jolene glanced up at me as if to say, *Uh oh, here we go again.* "We're both pretty. I mean, you're gorgeous, I'm pretty, and we both have awesome personalities. What's going on here?"

"Maybe it has to do with the fact that we were literary and film nerds in college. And that we frequented poetry slams." She shrugged. "We didn't exactly meet many guys outside of the classroom."

"Yeah." I looked over at her. "Any luck at work? Any hotties?"

"Meh." She shook her head. "No one I'm interested in losing my virginity to."

"Give it some time, you've only been there a week."

"Trust me, girl. I knew the first day." She laughed. "There are no potentials. Plus, all I'm doing is getting coffees and lunch orders right now. I'm the lowest of the low. No one is looking at me."

"I refuse to believe that." Lucy was one of the most gorgeous women I knew. With her long, naturally light blonde hair and dazzling green eyes, she had a face that was universally considered beautiful. Sometimes I was envious of the way she seemed to glow so naturally, while I had to use fake tan and bronzer to glow even a little. Even then, I sometimes ended up looking a little orange.

"Savannah, you're just as gorgeous as I am." She beamed at me. "And we're in the same boat, so it's got nothing to do with our looks."

"When I get a job, we're going out and painting the town red." I could already picture us out at the clubs, looking sexy and making men pant as we walked by. Okay, maybe not *pant*. Dogs panted, and the last thing I wanted was to be with a man who was a dog. I'd already dated a few of them. "And we will go to high-end, exclusive clubs and restaurants."

"Oh, yeah?" She laughed. "So, I take it you're getting a superb job then because I can't even afford to go to Shake Shack more than once a month right now."

"Don't worry. We have to have a positive mental attitude. This time next year, we will both be in awesome relationships, making a lot of money, and having the best sex of our lives."

"Well, it won't take much for us to have the best sex of our lives, considering our current status."

"Lucy, you overthink things too much."

I headed to our compact kitchen which was right next to the living room. In fact, some people might say that the kitchen and the living room were one and the same, seeing as they were both in the same room. On one side of the room, there was a small oven, a small fridge, a sink, two cupboards, and a little island separating the kitchen from the living room, which held our couch, a small coffee table, and two bookshelves filled with books and DVDs. The coffee table was pushed against the wall and also held a fairly large TV. I opened the fridge and grabbed a chocolate pudding and then a spoon. I pulled the top of the pudding off and licked the top before dropping it into the trashcan and heading back to the couch. Jolene looked at me hopefully as I dipped my spoon into the pudding and then gave me a dirty look as I shook my head. I loved my dog, but even I had to admit she was the greediest dog I'd ever met in my life.

Lucy crossed her arms. "Well, are you going to email and call about those jobs? I'm looking forward to this life of riches and excitement that you've promised me."

"Fine." I nodded. "Will you make some pasta for dinner?"

"But the pots?" She glanced at me and sighed. "Fine, I'll wash the dishes and make the dinner. You find yourself a job."

"Thanks, girl." I handed her my empty pudding container and spoon, and she rolled her eyes. I blew her a kiss, grabbed my laptop from the ground, and opened it up. I clicked on my email account and then grabbed the newspaper. I would email the six-figure job first and then I would call the other one. I much preferred to type than to talk. Even at poetry slams, I was always a little nervous speaking in public, and that was something I was good at. "Should I write a poem about why I'm good for the job?"

"Savannah Carter, shut the front door and get the hell out of town, are you joking me right now? No way, Jose! Do not write a poem for a job you're inquiring about!"

"Okay, okay!" I laughed, knowing that while I was smart, I still lacked what my mother called common sense and street smarts. Sometimes, I had such harebrained ideas that even I wondered what I was thinking. I stared at the ad again for the high six-figures job.

Do you want to earn high six-figures? Seeking professional for a unique job. Prefer MBA grad. Applicant would have to live in and wear a uniform. To apply, send resume and photograph to thewade@wade-hart.com.

Hmmm, I scratched a sudden itch on my back as I read the ad again. Why did they want a photograph? And what kind of job required a uniform? As much as I was interested in making a lot of money, I didn't want to do anything illegal or crazy. Well, not too crazy. I wouldn't dress up as a dominatrix and whip a man. Or would I? Would it really be that bad?

I resisted the urge to laugh at myself. I could tell myself that I would do a lot of things for money, but at the end of the day, I had my limits. Maybe I could whip a man for a month for a hundred grand … if I didn't also have to sleep with him. I would not sell my body. I wasn't some hooker. Though as the thought crossed my mind, I saw another ad that caught my interest.

"Lucy, there's an ad here that is looking for virgins. They will pay fifty grand to deflower you."

"Hell no!" Lucy looked over her shoulder at me as she scrubbed the pot I'd burned kidney beans into the night before. "We are not selling our virginity for fifty grand!"

"What if we auctioned it? I've heard of women doing that on eBay and stuff and getting, like, a million dollars." I held back a grin so she would think I was being serious.

"You'd move back to Florida and I'd move back to California before I let that happen." She rolled her eyes at me. "We want to lose our virginity to men we love, to passionate guys with six packs and dimples, not some old fat ass with bigger boobs than us and sagging balls."

"Who says the guys that buy our virginity are old and have sagging balls? Also, I don't really want a guy with a six-pack. You know I prefer a guy with more meat. I want a guy with muscles, yes, but not *too* muscular."

"Savannah, you are not selling your virginity to Billy Bob in Kentucky with no teeth and no hair."

"That's rude. I tell you, Kentucky has some hot-ass guys."

"They aren't bidding on your virginity ..." She raised an eyebrow at me and shook her head. "End of discussion. Apply to those jobs already, and then we can look online and see if we find any other suitable options."

"Yeah, because these options are so great ..." I said under my breath and turned back to my laptop and typed.

My mom always said if something sounds too good to be true, it is. But still, this was New York, and there were so many quirky millionaires and billionaires, maybe it would be legit.

To Whom It May Concern,

I would like to request more information about the assistant job I saw advertised in Sunday's newspaper with the high six-figure starting salary. I have a bachelor's degree in English and many years of work experience and I think I would be a suitable fit for the job. My questions are as follows:

1. What is the exact nature of the job?

2. Is it a strict requirement that I live with the boss? If so, can I have friends and others over?

3. The ad states there is a uniform. May I ask what sort of uniform? And why?

Also, in lieu of sending a photograph, I've sent a picture of my very friendly dog who would also join me if I were to get the job.

Yours sincerely,
　　　　Savannah Carter

I reread the email I'd sent and nodded. This sounded good, and the photo of Jolene was cute. Who could say no to living with her? I wanted to ask more questions but figured I'd wait for a response first. I hit send and then grabbed my phone to call about the other job. It rang twice before someone answered.

"Talia Enterprises, how may I help you?" The voice was sharp, but I tried to not let it dissuade me.

"Hello, my name is Savannah Carter. I'm calling about the job I saw advertised in the newspaper."

"Which one?"

"The sales job making six figures."

"Oh yes, yes, hold on, please." Before I could answer, the sound of music was playing in my ear. I debated hanging up the phone but stayed on the line. Just because the receptionist sounded like a bitch didn't mean that everyone at the company would be hostile and mean.

"Hello, Vanna, this is John Boy speaking."

"It's Savannah." His name was not really John Boy, was it?

"Yes, Vanna. How can I help you?"

"I was calling about the job."

"Which job?"

I withheld a sigh. "The sales job."

"Aw, great, great. This is an awesome opportunity. Totally awesome. For the right person. High salary. Great benefits. There's a lot of money to be made."

"Well, that sounds great." I could feel myself perking up. "So, can I get some more information?"

"Of course, of course." He sounded overly friendly now. "We are the fastest-growing company in the last five years. I started in sales myself, and now I'm a manager. Yup, yup. Very great company. I think you will love it. Great opportunity and lots of money. If you have expensive tastes, you will want to work here."

"Hmm, okay, but uhm, what exactly do you sell, and what would my job be? What kind of sales?"

"Have you ever sold anything before?" he asked me cheerfully. "Doesn't matter if you haven't, of course, we will train you. All training is provided in our state-of-the-art office in New Jersey. Where do you live?"

"I'm in Manhattan."

"Oh, okay, well, just a train ride away. We're in Jersey City. You can see the skyline from Jersey City, did you know that? Great bang for your buck."

"Uhm, okay. And what do you sell again?"

"Do you have a lot of friends? Or any friends looking for a job? Or a great investment opportunity?"

"Investment opportunity?" I wrinkled my nose and looked over to Lucy who was smiling at me, looking hopeful once again. I knew it worried her that we'd be kicked out if I couldn't find my half of the rent, so I tried to ignore the warning bells ringing in my head. "What do you mean?"

"Oh, nothing, nothing. Can you come for an interview tomorrow morning? Around ten a.m."

"Yes. Yes, I can."

"Okay great, bring your photo ID and social security card and bank account information so we can fill out the paperwork."

"The paperwork?"

"So you can get started as soon as possible."

"But I don't have the job yet."

"Oh, I can tell you will be a great fit at Talia Enterprises, the interview is just a formality. I'll see you tomorrow. Just google Talia Enterprises New Jersey for our address. Once you arrive, ask for John Boy and I'll come and take you to my office."

"Do you have a last name, John Boy, or is it Walton?"

"Sorry what?" He sounded confused. "Why do you want to know my last name? Who do you work for? You're not with the SEC, are you?"

"What?" It was my turn to sound confused. "I don't work for anyone. That's why I'm applying for this job. I was making a joke because the only John Boy I know was in *The Waltons*."

"I don't follow the Walmart family, sorry."

"What?" I closed my mouth as it fell open. "*The Waltons* is an old TV show. Maybe you never saw it? Sorry, I grew up with it. My mom loved to make me watch the shows she grew up with."

"Okay, well, good, good. See you tomorrow. Oh, and we have a business casual policy, so dress to impress. Goodbye, Vanna." And with that, he hung up the phone.

I stared at my black screen for a few seconds and I didn't know whether to laugh or cry.

"Well, I have some good-ish news." I stood up and walked over to the kitchen. "I think I might have a job. Bad news is, the hiring manager sounds like he's out of his mind, but hopefully, I won't be working under him."

"Congratulations, are you going to take it, then?" Lucy beamed happily. "Did he say what the salary was?"

"Nope, he just said it was high, and that there was a lot of room for growth. But he also asked if I had friends interested in investment opportunities." I bit down on my lower lip. "What the hell does that mean?"

"Oh, I bet they're looking for investors so they can expand." Lucy shrugged.

"Expand what and into where?"

"I don't know. Maybe ask tomorrow." She did a little dance. "This is so exciting. You know what this means, right?"

"No, what?"

"Tonight, we open the bottle of wine I got at Whole Foods last week. Let's celebrate."

"Do you really think we should celebrate already?" I stared at my phone screen. "I don't have the job yet."

"Okay, fine, we can celebrate tomorrow."

"Ooh, I got a reply from the other job already." I opened my email account up and read the response quickly. "Hmm, this guy sounds like a jerk."

"Why what did he say?"

"Listen to this." I cleared my throat and then read his email.

M*s. Carter,*

. . .

How do you know you'll be a suitable fit for the job if you do not know the nature of the work? My ad specifically stated I was looking for an MBA grad, not an English grad who knows nothing about the real world.

1. This would be discussed in the interview.

2. Yes, you would live with me. And no guests are allowed.

3. The uniform would be provided on your first day. You don't need to know why.

The job advertisement asked for a personal photo, is this your way of telling me you look like a dog?

Today must be your lucky day because you're the only person that responded to my ad. Are you available for a phone interview tomorrow?

The Wade Hart

"Who the hell calls themselves *The* anything. What a pompous jerk."

"Is he famous?" Lucy asked, sounding curious.

"I don't know, let me check." I opened the internet browser on my phone and typed in *Wade Hart*. Several thousand results came up for the name so I then typed in wade-hart.com, but no website showed up. "There are too many listings for Wade Hart, but none of them seem famous."

"Check out the photos and see if any look cute."

"Lucy, even if I saw cute photos, I wouldn't know if it was him, and who even cares? He essentially just called me a dog." I shook my head and closed my phone. "I think I'll pass on Mr. Wade Hart. I basically have this job tomorrow, and even if my boss is a douche, I'll suck it up for a few months to make some money, and then I'll get a new job or something." I nodded. "I mean it's a job. It's like you said, something is better than nothing."

My stomach growled just then, and I rubbed it pitifully, hoping that dinner would be ready soon. I had a sinking feeling, but I was hoping it had more to do with the fact that I was hungry than the fact that I still did not understand exactly what sales I'd be doing once I hit New Jersey.

CHAPTER 2

I checked my reflection in the tiny compact mirror Lucy had gotten for me in Florence and decided I looked smart and professional. I had on my best navy-blue suit and black pumps, and my hair was tied in a loose bun at the top of my head. I took a deep breath, placed my compact back in my handbag, licked my lips, and walked into the office building in front of me. There was a small silver sign next to the number that read *Talia Enterprises,* so I knew I was in the right location, even if nothing else about the building looked that professional. I walked through the doors and headed to the check-in desk where an old man sat with earphones in.

"Well, I was telling Jimmy, put a hundred on it for me. If Prince Caspian comes in first, I'll make five hundred bucks, and I told Jimmy I'm good for it." He was talking quickly.

"Hello, I'm here for—" I began, but he held his hand up to stop me.

"I even told him I would split the winnings with him. And do you know what that bastard said to me? He said *no.*" The man started coughing, and I looked around to see if there was anyone else that could help me.

I spoke up again. "Excuse me, but I have an interview and—"

"Lady, I'm on the phone." He looked annoyed. "So, Jimmy doesn't place the bet and Caspian comes in and I called him and I said, look, you could have been ..."

As the man continued talking, I looked around the small, decrepit-looking lobby and saw an elevator. I walked away from the man and headed towards the elevator.

"Lady, you can't go in there, sign in first," the man called from behind me, but I didn't even bother turning back. There was no way I would be late for my interview because I was listening to him talk about horse racing. I pressed the button and walked into the elevator, willing my nerves to subside as I pressed the button to take me to the fourth floor, where Talia Enterprises was located according to the sign next to the numbers.

A moment later, the ding of the bell alerted me to the fact that I had arrived on the fourth floor. I plastered on an enormous smile as I stepped out into the hallway. Directly across from the elevator was a wide-open door through which I could hear the bustle of people chatting. I headed to the door and peered in.

"Hello?" I stepped inside.

"Hey, what's up?" A young guy with a green mohawk looked at me with a smile.

"I'm here to see John Boy. About a job?"

"Oh, okay, cool. Cool." He grinned and walked over to me. "I'm Andrew."

"Nice to meet you. I'm Savannah."

"Savannah. Cool. Cool." He nodded. "I guess that's better than marsh or desert."

"Sorry, what?"

"A savannah is a grassy plain in a tropical region with few trees." He sounded as if he'd recently memorized that information for a test. "Better you were named for that type of topography. Though I think it would be cool to be called—"

"Uhm, is John Boy here?" I interrupted him. "I'm here for an interview, and I don't want him to think I'm late."

"Sure, sure. Hold on." He turned around and then shouted, "John Boy, come to the front, some chick is here to see you!" He turned back to me and nodded. "That should do it." He picked his nose and then grinned at me. "Good luck, you'll enjoy working here."

"Thank you," I said as he walked away, trying to hide my disgust. Every bone in my body was screaming and begging me to run as quickly as possible. This place was like the Twilight Zone, and not in a good way. Who the hell were these people? I looked around the room as I waited for John Boy to join me. To my left, there was a table of about three women on phones with stacks of papers in front of them. Sitting behind them stood Andrew and another guy who were placing small packages into individual boxes. I was about to ask them what they were doing when a slim man with big blue eyes hurried towards me.

"Vanna, there you are." He held out his hand to greet me. "So glad you could make it. I'm sure you must be excited to start today."

"To start?" I blinked. "Uhm, I thought I was here for an interview?"

"Well, I considered our phone call yesterday the interview, this is your first day. Congratulations." He nodded. "This is a marvelous opportunity for you. Very marvelous and very great. There's lots of money to be made here. Lots and lots of money."

"About that … What's the salary?"

"You'll find our compensation scheme is very, very generous." He nodded. "You won't be disappointed. Let's go to my office and we can discuss."

"Uhm, okay." I followed behind him and as we passed Andrew, I looked down at the plastic bags. Each bag contained a hairbrush, comb, and hairspray. "And you'll tell me exactly what the position is? Sorry, but I feel like I don't even know what the job is."

"Don't worry, you'll be great. Maybe you'll be a manager by next month." John Boy's fingers seemed to twitch, and I wanted to tell him he still had answered none of my questions. We finally made it into his office, which, to be fair, looked nice with its large wooden desk and iMac computer. "Have a seat." He nodded to the leather chair, and I sat down as he walked to his seat on the other side of the desk. "So, will you be using a credit card or check today?"

"What?"

"We take Visa, Mastercard, American Express, Discover," he smiled widely. "And checks."

"I didn't bring any checks, but I noted my routing and account information ..." I frowned. "I can fill that in when I fill out the payroll info, though. I didn't know you could pay people through their credit cards."

"Oh, we will give you checks. The credit card is for the payment you're making today."

"Payment for what?" Sweat started to trickle down the back of my neck.

"Well, that's up to you. Would you prefer to be a bronze, silver, gold, or platinum employee?" He beamed at me. "All of them are great, but obviously you'll make more money when you start off at a higher level."

"Start off with what?" My fingers clutched the side of my bag. What the hell was he talking about?

"Well, as you can see, we are the number-one retailer for top-quality hairbrushes, combs, and sprays, and our packets go for the cheap price of $25. We try to sell our packs to stores and hairdressers across the country."

"Uhm, okay ..." I bit down on my lower lip. "And so what would my role be?"

"Well, you would be the most important person in the company. Your role in sales would have you cold-calling customers to make appointments to show our first-class goods. Then you will take them directly to the customers' houses and sell them. We have several other products you can upsell them with to make even more money."

"Okay." My heart was racing now and my brain was wondering if I could run out of his office without him catching me. "So, what's with the different levels?"

"Well, obviously we can't just trust you with the products. You choose a starting level of products to buy and sell. As an employee, you will receive a discount, so you can buy the packets at $20 and sell them for whatever you want."

"You want *me* to buy the products I'm supposed to sell for you?" My jaw dropped. "What?"

"And if you have any friends or family who might be interested in this amazing investment opportunity, you get a discount. So, each friend you refer that signs up to be a sales-person gives you $1 off each package." He grinned. "For life."

"Is there a salary as well?" My voice trailed off. I wasn't even sure why I was asking, there was no way I was working here.

"Of course." He held up a laminated sheet. "If you start at our platinum level, your buy-in is $5000, but you will start at $6 an hour. The $6 is earned by you going through our lists and calling to make appointments for all our sales-people. Also, you will help to pack the bags. You have to work a minimum of twenty hours here in the office, but the rest of the time you can spend in the field, selling."

"Oh, okay." I didn't know what else to say. I was torn between tears and hysterical laughter. I was hoping he'd say, "Joke, I got ya, you're on a hidden camera TV show!" or something, but I knew that wasn't about to happen. I'd come all the way to Jersey for a pyramid scheme and not even a very good one at that. "Uhm, so I think that I will have to pass on this opportunity." I stood up. "I heard back from someone else and, uh, that job seems more suited to me."

I didn't wait for him to respond and hurried out of his office and towards the entrance. My heart was racing, and I almost ran into the elevator when it arrived. I took two deep breaths and grabbed my phone to call Lucy. She would totally laugh when I told her this story. This didn't even feel like real life. Only I would respond to an ad for a "job" like this.

I ran out of the elevator when it arrived on the first floor and it wasn't a surprise to see the security guard still chatting on the phone as I exited the building. He didn't even look up at me as I hurried out. I should have known when I'd seen him that that entire thing would be a fiery mess.

"How did it go?" Lucy answered on the first ring. I groaned loudly in response. "Uh oh, that bad?"

"Worse."

"What were you selling?"

"You don't want to know!"

"Sex toys?"

"I wish." I laughed. "Girl, I will tell you when I get home. I'm so depressed. This sucks."

"Why don't you reply to that other job, then?"

"I guess so, it literally can't be worse than the nightmare I'm just leaving."

"Oh, I can't wait to hear more."

"Trust me, you will laugh all night long." I sighed. "I'll see you at home? I need to run to the train and then I will email The Wade Hart back." I chewed on my lower lip for a few seconds. "I just pray to God that this is a genuine job and not some bullshit scheme. Telling me I can earn six-figures by donating six-figures or something."

"What?"

"Nothing. I'll tell you later." I laughed, feeling better just hearing her voice. "I hope your day is going better than mine. See you later."

I hung up and ran my fingers through my hair and shook my head. I had never expected that life would be so hard after college. I'd thought once I'd gotten into Columbia, my entire life would just be amazing. I had never expected that I'd graduate without a job and mountains of debt. And even if I wanted my parents to help, they couldn't. My dad worked for a small paper in Brevard County and my mom had been a stay-at-home parent, taking care of me and my younger brother. My dad still worked, but he didn't make much money. And he was helping my brother pay for college at UCF. There was no way I could ask him to help me out. My only options were finding a job to help me pay my bills or moving back home. And as much as I'd loved Palm Bay, I was in no hurry to go back. I'd respond to Mr. Hart and see how I felt about the job after the interview. And if push came to shove, I'd get a job waitressing in a restaurant or something.

CHAPTER 3

To Whom It May Concern,

I am available for a phone interview. I would like to know what the job comprises, though. I do not look like a dog, and I don't appreciate the sentiment. Also, I'm not sure that I would say today was my lucky day just because you gave me an interview. To be honest, wouldn't you say that it was your lucky day, seeing as I was the only one that was interested in the job?

Yours sincerely,
Savannah Carter

I read my response over. I knew that I sounded bitchy, but I really didn't care. There was also no way I was addressing my email to The Wade Hart. I'd keep it as formal as possible, and if this was a serious job, they would understand that. I pressed send before I could change my mind. I sat back in my seat as the train made its way from the station and scrolled through the calendar on my favorite coffee shop's website. There was a poetry slam coming up on

Friday, and I figured that it would be a fun activity for Lucy and me to attend where we could let off some steam. I'd have to write something new, though. I opened the notebook app on my phone and waited for inspiration to hit.

Ping.

A new email alert appeared, and I opened it quickly. It was a response from The Wade Hart.

Dear Ms. Carter,
    Are you available for a call now? I expected a response last night, but I can fit you in for an interview right now. What's your phone number? I didn't say you look like a dog. You did. Today was not my lucky day. Well, not yet at least. Let's see what happens tonight.

My name isn't To Whom It May Concern. It's Wade Hart. Have you ever sent cover and/or informative letters for a job before?

The Wade Hart

I stared at his response and rolled my eyes. This guy sounded like a jerk. When the hell had I said I look like a dog? And what was he insinuating by saying that tonight might be his lucky night? Was he talking about sex? My face flushed. This kind of inappropriateness was out of control, but I needed this job. I needed a genuine job that paid me, and paid me quickly. Rent was due soon, and I had no other options right now. I regretfully responded to his email with my number and closed my eyes. Panic and anxiety flooded me and I tried to take a few deep breaths. My fingers felt sweaty, and as my phone started ringing, I dropped it onto the ground. My eyes popped open quickly, and I grabbed the phone and answered it, ignoring the rude stare of the elderly lady sitting across from me.

"Hello, this is Savannah Carter."

"Savannah, this is Wade Hart." A smooth silky voice sounded in my ear and it surprised me at how much the sound delighted me. He sounded hot, arrogant but super-hot, if a voice could sound hot.

"You mean, *The* Wade Hart?" I couldn't stop myself from responding and I froze as my comment was met with silence. Oh, shit—had I blown the interview already? And then he chuckled, a warm, delicious sound that made my stomach flip.

"Yes, *the* Wade Hart." He cleared this throat. "I'm guessing this is who let the dogs out, Savannah Carter?"

"You can just call me Ms. Carter."

"Maybe I want to call you Savannah."

"That works, sir."

"How did you know my favored title?" He chuckled, and I rolled my eyes. I looked around the train and I could tell that the older lady across from me was listening to my conversation.

"I made a good guess," I said and then realized that I was not going about this the right way if I wanted the job. "But I will call you whatever you want, Mr. Hart. I was hoping you would tell me more about the job."

"You'd be my personal assistant. Have you ever been a personal assistant before?"

"Uhm ..." I hadn't, but I wasn't sure if I would stand a chance if I said no. "Not in a professional capacity, but while I was in college, I helped to TA a class and was the assistant to one of my professors." That was a bit of a stretch. I'd helped to collect tests at the end of one of our exams, but I would not tell Wade Hart that.

"And your resume says you went to Columbia."

"Yes, yes, I did. Graduated with a 3.8 GPA."

"So, not a perfect 4.0?"

"No." I bit down on my lower lip. "Where did you go to college?"

"Harvard undergrad, Wharton for business school," he said smoothly. "I studied economics."

"So, you work in finance?"

"Did I say that?"

"Not exactly, but I suppose I made a guess based upon what you told me."

"So you assumed?"

"Yes, I assumed you were in finance."

"They know what they say when you assume something ..." There was a light tone to his voice, and I realized he was teasing me. I wondered if he would actually complete that sentence. Was he really going to say you make an ass out of you and me? If he did, I would hang up right now. I would hang up the phone, go home, sleep, and hopefully wake up in a new and less cliched reality.

"No, I don't know."

"Hmm, well, they say you shouldn't do it." I said a silent prayer as he didn't complete the juvenile saying. "I dabble in the stock market, but I'm actually more focused on trade in emerging markets."

"Uhm, okay." What the hell was he talking about?

"I'm involved in a lot of import and export and supporting third-world economies with sustainable businesses."

"That sounds wonderful." I still did not understand what that meant, but I would not tell him that.

"I need an assistant who can be on-site with me for the next six months."

"May I ask why? Where do you live? Can't I just commute to work?"

"I live outside the city. And no, you can't just commute to work. Given the nature of the job, we will work at different hours of the day. Some days, we might start at 3 a.m., some at noon. I need you on hand at all times."

"Oh, hmmm." I couldn't really argue with the time-zone logic. "And I'd be paid a salary? And be given my own place?"

"You'll be living in my house, and you would have your own room." He said. "Given how often and quickly I will need your services, it makes no sense for you to not be on the property. And of course, you will have a salary. I don't expect you to work for free."

"And what is the salary, and does the job only last six months?"

"The first assignment is for six months. If we work well together, I will extend it. You will receive three lump sums of a hundred thousand dollars. One payment on acceptance of the job, the second payment at month three, and the last payment at the end of the six months."

"That's a lot of money for six months." My mom's words hit me again, if something sounds too good to be true, it usually was.

"It is, but you will work a lot. Some weeks you might work a hundred hours, and I will need for you to do everything I ask when I ask." He sounded serious. "You will work hard. I need someone that can commit to doing everything I require of them when I require it."

"What will you be requiring of me?" *Please God, do not say I will have to go door-to-door selling plastic brushes and combs.*

"You will facilitate meetings between me and different world leaders and corporation directors, you will create PowerPoint presentations, you will create graphics and videos for ads on social media, and you will write press releases. There will also be some travel where we will set up different site locations, and you will be in charge of quality control for the different products. You will also be in charge of cataloging all of said products, you will be responsible for the weekly grocery shopping and menus for lunch and dinner. I can take care of my breakfast." He paused. "Those would be some of your duties."

"Okay, well, just so I know." Was he joking? That sounded like a laundry load of duties. Much more than one person could handle.

"I know that it sounds like a lot, and I know that you might wonder why I'm not hiring multiple people. I do not trust people. I believe in the saying, too many cooks in the kitchen spoil the pot. I need one person who can do everything I require, and that is why the salary is so high."

"Hmm," I bit down on my lower lip. I didn't even know how to do half of the duties he was asking of me, but I knew that the salary sounded amazing and what was six months? Nothing. I could pay off a significant amount of debt. I could pay my rent.

"Also, I know you most probably have a place in the city, I would cover that rent while you were upstate with me working."

"You will? On top of my salary?"

"Yes. And of course, I will provide all meals."

"Wow, okay, that sounds great."

"I know it is a generous offer." He paused again. "Now I need to ask you some questions. Please tell me about your previous work experience. I know you studied English in college, but that will only be helpful for the press releases, not any of your other duties."

"Well, obviously I don't have a wealth of experience seeing as I just graduated from college, but I'm smart and a go-getter. Some of my previous duties in different jobs included creating PowerPoint presentations, balancing different bank accounts and reconciling the numbers, shopping for the elderly, making phone calls to different law enforcement and federal agencies about defective consumer products ..." I took a deep breath, trying to think of other creative ways to talk about my past.

"Let's be honest here, Ms. Carter, that all sounds like a lot of bullshit." He cleared his throat. "From what I can tell, you're not even remotely qualified for this job, but I do like the way you have tried to make your lack of work history sound like more than it is. You can spin a web, and I need someone willing to spin and weave whatever I tell them too."

"I don't know if I should be happy or offended by your statement."

"Be happy. There's no point wasting time being offended by the truth. I need you to start tomorrow. I'll email you a train ticket. You'll leave from Penn Station."

"But I haven't even accepted the job! Plus, you don't know if I can leave tomorrow."

"Send me your checking account details tonight via email and I'll wire you the first payment of a hundred grand tomorrow morning."

"Like I said, I haven't even decided if I want the job."

"The mere fact that you answered my ad and that you're on the phone with me right now tells me you want and need this job, Ms. Carter. I don't like playing games, so please don't start playing any now."

"I'm not playing any games."

"Find someone to look after your mutt and pack your bags tonight. The train will leave at 7 a.m. Be prepared to work when you arrive. I'll have you picked up at the station."

"You mean you don't expect me to pick myself up?"

"You have a sense of humor. To be honest, that's one of the reasons why you're getting the job."

"Why, thank you. I always knew my personality would work for me one day."

"Are you going to send me your photo now?"

"Nope. Are you going to send me one?"

"Are you scared you won't get the job because you're ugly?"

"Are you scared I won't accept the job because you look like a troll?"

"I can assure you that I don't look like a troll, Ms. Carter, far from it."

"Uh huh."

"You're twenty-one?"

"No, I'm twenty-two, and I'm fairly certain it's illegal to ask me my age in a job interview."

He chuckled. "You already have the job. I'm making a personal inquiry."

"Sure." Even though I could tell the man was insufferable, I quite liked the sparring that we did. I'd never met or spoken to a man like this before. "How old are you?"

"I'm thirty."

"Old, then."

"You think thirty is old?"

"Well, it's not young, is it?"

"I can tell that you're a woman that enjoys a good spanking."

"Excuse me?" My jaw dropped. "What did you just say to me?"

"My apologies, you're right. I misspoke. I should have said, you're a woman that deserves a good spanking. I don't know if you enjoy it or not."

My heart started racing then because I hadn't expected the conversation to turn this inappropriate already. Who the hell was this guy? And why the hell did I want to work for him?

Well, I *didn't* want to work for him, but I wanted the salary. Shit, the money would solve all my immediate problems. But not if he turned out to be a crazy man. If I ended up locked up and or dead, the money wouldn't matter.

"Look, Mr. Hart, I'm not sure what you're saying, but I just want to make sure that this job is legit. Do you have any references I can call? I can't just catch a train and go upstate and live with you without having even met you." I cleared my throat nervously. "And I'm not sure what you're saying about the spanking? You're not looking for some sex arrangement, are you?" I tried to lower my voice as the last words because the older lady was practically gawking at me now.

"I don't need you for sex, and I have no interest in paying someone for a sexual arrangement." He laughed. "Far from it. You need not worry. I will send you a reference to check. The head of a reputable hedge fund on Wall Street, he will vouch for me."

"We'll see."

"I have to go now, Ms. Carter, but if you're serious about making some money, I expect to receive your bank account info tonight and I'll see you first thing tomorrow."

"That doesn't even leave me much time to—" My voice trailed off as he hung up.

I sat there just staring at the phone. Had he really just hung up on me? I waited for the phone to light up to show he was calling again, but nothing happened.

My brain went into overdrive. It was a lot of money, but something about the situation made the hairs on the back of my neck stand up. Nonetheless, I was such an idiot that I was excited as well as scared by the possibility of working with him. What did he look like? Was he a hottie? And why would it matter, anyway? It wasn't as if I was going there to date him. I would be his assistant, his subordinate. I would be kissing his ass more than his face.

I was about to email him to let him know that I would not take the job when a text came through from Lucy.

Hate to scare you, but the landlord just called. Rent is going up $400 starting next month. Might have to call my dad. Ugh. Good luck with the interview. I hope you get the job because we need some good luck.

Fuck it. I would have to take the job. I'd hit up a camping store tonight and buy a knife to take with me. If Mr. Wade Hart tried anything with me, I'd cut off his balls, or at least puncture a rib or something as I made my getaway. I needed this job and this money. I knew Lucy didn't want to call her dad. He wasn't happy about her internship. She'd been the best and most supportive friend I ever could have asked for, so I'd suck it up and work at this job for six months.

And maybe, just maybe, it wouldn't be as bad as I expected it would be.

CHAPTER 4

"Savannah, you cannot take this job. The guy sounds deranged." Lucy grabbed the shirt in my hand and hid it behind her back. "I refuse to let you catch a train and go to some unknown town in the middle of nowhere."

"It's two hours out of the city, Lucy." I tried to grab my shirt back from her. "And it will be fine. I called the reference he gave me, and it was legit. He might be an asshole, but he's a real businessman."

"This sounds like the beginning of a movie on Lifetime." She glared at me as she stepped back. "If you go missing and a hot cop comes and asks me where you went, I will scream."

"I won't go missing, and no hot cops are going to come asking you anything. You will never talk to a hot cop unless you go to a police station to find one."

"Yeah, I'll be like, arrest me, officer, I've been a bad girl."

"Lucy!" I giggled at her. "Can I have my shirt back please?"

"Fine, but I don't like it. Why do you have to start tomorrow?"

"I guess he needs someone right away." I shrugged as she

handed me back my shirt and I folded it and put it into my suitcase. "You're sure you don't mind taking care of Jolene while I'm gone?"

"I don't mind." I could tell from her face that she had concerns, but I didn't say anything. It would mean she'd have to come home for lunch to walk Jolene, but right now we didn't have many options. "You sure you can't take her?"

"Well, Wade said that he didn't want me to bring her." I was thoughtful for a moment. "But can he reasonably expect that I'm not going to bring my dog. Who does he think I'm going to get to look after her in one evening?"

"Exactly! What's he going to say? You're fired?"

"Possibly." I stared at my suitcase full of clothes. "He really knows nothing about me, and I know nothing about him. He might take one look at me and be like, on your bike, go back to the city."

"If he let you keep the hundred grand, that wouldn't be so bad."

"Yeah, wouldn't it? Oh, my phone's ringing." I turned around to figure out which stack of clothes it was hiding under and grabbed it quickly, frowning when I saw Wade's name on the screen. "This is Savannah Carter, how may I help you?"

"Savannah, this is Sir." I could tell from the humor in his voice that he wanted me to react, but I wasn't going to give him that satisfaction.

"Why hello, sir. How may I help you this good evening?"

"I just wanted to make sure you got the train information."

"I did."

"Good, you'll arrive at 11:23, look for a guy holding a sign with your name on it."

"Okay."

"I received your bank account info and you should see the first deposit in your account after midnight."

"Thank you."

"Don't go spending it all at once."

"Maybe I'll just skip the train and go shopping tomorrow."

"I wouldn't do that if I were you."

"Oh, yeah?"

"Yes. Sir wouldn't be happy."

"But how would The Wade Hart feel about it?"

I could see Lucy staring at me with narrowed eyes as she listened to my side of the conversation. I was certain that she was about to rip all of my clothes out of my suitcase and dump them on the floor and forbid me to go if she heard more of the conversation.

"He wouldn't be happy. He might have to come into the city to tell you off, and that would make him mad. And you don't want to see him when he's mad."

"Do you always talk in the third person? And I've never seen you period, so frankly, I don't care if you're mad, happy, sad—you name the emotion, I don't care."

"You're being fairly mouthy for someone I'm employing with a huge salary."

"Would it be better if I wasn't making a huge salary?" I asked innocently. I couldn't believe just how snappy I was being.

"Savannah Carter, you have no idea who you're talking to."

"No, I know exactly who I'm talking to."

"Get to the train station early tomorrow, and don't forget to bring a bathing suit with you."

"A bathing suit?"

"That's what I said."

"Why do I need a bathing suit?"

"Because I enjoy going on morning swims."

"So? What does that have to do with me?"

"You'll be joining me. I enjoy racing."

"You don't even know if I can swim."

"Well, if you can't, don't bother getting on the train."

"What?"

"Don't bother getting on the train."

"You can't do that."

"I haven't paid you everything yet, you haven't signed any contracts. I can do what I want."

"Whatever."

"Can you swim?"

"Maybe."

"Bring the suit, and I'll see you tomorrow." He paused and chuckled. "In fact, I'm quite looking forward to it." Once again, he hung up the phone without even having the courtesy to say goodbye.

"He wants me to bring my bathing suit." I looked at Lucy and shook my head, the shock of the call finally hitting me. "So we can go for morning swims."

"What the hell?" Lucy sat on the couch and played with her hair. "Are you really sure you still want to go?"

"It will only be for six months. I can last that long." I nodded. "Plus, I want to put this guy in his place. He needs to know that he can't speak to people like that."

"What bathing suit are you going to take? A one-piece or a two-piece?"

"How about a no-piece." I laughed. "He can swim by himself. He can't make me swim and race him in the mornings."

"But you love swimming." Lucy looked surprised. "You were the star of your swim team in high school."

"I was *on* the swim team. I was nowhere near the star," I

reminded her. "But my parents had a pool, and I grew up swimming, so I was a natural."

"Are you going to tell him that?"

"Oh, hell no." I shook my head. "The less he knows about my life, the better. I'm going there to do a job, and I'll do the real work to the best of my ability, but if he has any bullshit requests for me, I'm going to tell him where he can shove it."

"Oh Savannah, are you sure?" Lucy stood up and walked over to me before grabbing my shoulders. "You call me if you need anything, you hear? Absolutely anything."

"I will."

"I'll miss you." She leaned in and gave me a huge hug. "And Jolene and I are going to come up and visit soon. I don't care if he says you can't have visitors. We'll rent a place and stay for a weekend. He has to give you time off."

"That sounds amazing. I can't wait." I hugged her back tightly and as I pulled back, I looked into her eyes and gave her a wry smile. "At least I'll have something to write about. I'll be killing the slams when I'm back."

"Yes, yes, you will." She nodded and looked at the mess on the floor. "Now let's finish getting you packed so that we can go and have that farewell drink before it gets too late."

"Sounds like a plan."

I grabbed a handful of panties and put them in the side of my suitcase, the nerves in my stomach twirling and whirling with anticipation and excitement. There was something about Wade that intrigued me. He was obviously not going to be like any boss I'd ever had before. I hadn't even met him and he'd already crossed multiple boss-employee lines. I wondered what he looked like. Would he be tall? Short? Blonde, redhead, brunette? What color eyes did he have? What was his background? Was he handsome? Did he have a nice body? A long cock? My face grew red as the last thought hit me. Why was I thinking about his cock? Was I that desperate to get laid that some unknown man intrigued me just because he had a hot voice?

No, I knew it was more than that. There was something naughty, even erotic about our conversations. Some part of me wondered if this job was the gateway to being his sex slave. The idea was ridiculous, but I knew it wasn't out of the realm of possibility. Not that I would tell Lucy that, though. She'd think I'd read too many books or seen too many sexy movies. No, I'd keep my thoughts to myself. Once I got there, I would decide how to handle the situation I found myself in.

Wade Hart might be calling the shots now, but he was in for a surprise if he thought I was just going to do whatever he wanted without asking why.

CHAPTER 5

As I sipped my lukewarm cup of coffee, I realized I should have grabbed another packet of sugar. The coffee was bitter, and I really didn't want to finish it, but I knew if I didn't, I would be too tired when I arrived, and the last thing I wanted was to be yawning when I met Wade. Not that he didn't deserve to think he was boring. He totally did, but I also knew that I wanted and needed this job. I couldn't afford to give him a reason to fire me on the first day. Wade lived in a town called Herne Hill Village. I'd never heard of it before, but I was excited to visit after looking at photos online. I stared out of the window as the train chugged along, and I knew immediately when we'd left the outskirts of the city. Gone were the tall skyscrapers and buildings built upon each other. The landscape in front of me was lush and green, and every now and then I saw a row of houses with plants and tall trees that made me smile. It always surprised me just how small New York City was. It hadn't taken very long at all for me to find myself in what felt like a whole new world.

"Next stop is Herne Hill Village." The conductor announced, and I gathered my stuff together. This was it, then. I was about to start my new job. About to meet a man who I already knew would infuriate me.

About to arrive. I'll text later and tell you how it goes. I quickly typed a message to Lucy and hit send. I knew she'd be waiting for text later in anticipation. I jumped up out of my seat and held onto the rail as the train slowed down. Then I grabbed my suitcase and made my way off of the train and towards the small station. My legs felt slightly wobbly as I walked. Only about five other people had gotten off the train at this stop, and all of them seemed to know exactly where they were going. I walked through the door and looked around to see if I could see anyone. There was no one waiting for me. No chauffeur with a sign with my name. No nothing. I stood there for a few moments, my heart thudding, and wondered if I should call Wade to see what was going on.

What if this is a sign, Savannah? Maybe I wasn't meant to be here. Maybe I should buy a ticket and catch the next train back to New York City. I looked around the station for the ticket counter and was about to make some inquiries when a man ran in through the main entrance, a white card in his hand. He looked around, spotted me, and raced up to me with a grin, his light green eyes radiating mischief as he looked me over.

"Savannah Carter?" he asked. I nodded in response. "So sorry I'm late, I stopped to get a bagel and it took forever." He looked down at my lone suitcase. "Is that all you have with you?"

"Yes."

"Wow." He looked impressed. "I've had girlfriends pack two suitcases just for a weekend trip to the Hamptons." He laughed and then he ran his hand through his short dark brown hair. "I'm Henry, by the way, nice to meet you."

"Hello, Henry." I shook his hand, and he grabbed my suitcase.

"Follow me, I brought the Range Rover today because I thought you'd have a lot of baggage. If I'd known you didn't, I would have taken you out for a spin in the Bugatti."

"Oh, okay." Who was this guy?

"The estate is about an hour and a half away," he continued. "We're pretty isolated, no shops or anything within walking distance. Are you hungry? We can pick something up for the ride back."

"If you don't think Mr. Hart will mind."

"Oh, who cares what Wade thinks?" He threw back his head and laughed. "What's he going to say? You can't eat?"

"Well, you know him better than me ..." I debated asking him my next question then decided to get it out of the way. "Is he a good boss?"

"Good boss?" Henry shrugged. "Hell if I know. I doubt it. Not with his temper." He seemed to realize he'd said the wrong thing and then smiled a wide smile at me. "But I'm sure he'll be great."

"You don't work for him?"

"Work for him?" He laughed as if I'd told the funniest joke ever. "No, never!" He stopped and looked at me with a sly smile. "I'm Henry Hart, I'm Wade's younger, better-looking brother." He grinned, a cocky boyish smile that was charming and infectious. "Don't tell him I said that, though."

"Oh, I didn't realize you were his brother, sorry."

"No need to be sorry." We stopped next to a black Range Rover and he opened the trunk. "Why else would I be picking you up if I didn't work for Wade?" He shook his head. "Not that I have my own life or anything." He lifted up my suitcase and slammed the trunk shut. "It's Wade's world, and we just live in it."

"Funny." I smiled at him. "So, do you live with him, then? At the estate?"

"Oh, God no." We walked to the passenger side of the SUV and he opened the door for me. "I'm just visiting for a week. He asked me to do him a favor and pick you up because he's on some important call with the president of some country in Africa."

"Wow."

"He takes his work very seriously." He shrugged. "Which is good for me and for him. He runs the family business, and the profits go to my trust fund, so I can't complain."

"Is the house very large, then?"

"Yes, it's massive." He grinned as I got inside the car and then closed the door. I buckled my seatbelt and watched as he got into the car. He looked over at me and studied my face. "You're pretty young, aren't you? To be taking a job all the way out here."

"It seemed like a good opportunity."

"No boyfriend?"

"No." I shook my head, not offended by his question. Henry was handsome, and I was curious if he had a girlfriend.

"You seem sensible." He smiled. "Yes, you seem like a girl with principles."

"Sorry, what?"

"Nothing." He shook his head and smiled. "You just don't look like the sort of woman who can be swayed by a dollar."

"I'm not sure what that means."

"It means that soon I could be the owner of a Lamborghini Veneno." He grinned as he started the engine. "I'm still debating if I want it in black or red."

"Oh, okay, cool."

"I'll give you a piece of advice before we arrive. My

brother is a bit of a hard-ass, but just because he's your boss, don't feel like you have to do everything that he asks you to do."

"Oh, trust me, I won't." I shook my head. "I might need this job to pay my rent and student loans, but I'm not here to be his maid or bootlicker."

"Bootlicker?" Henry gave me a look as we drove off. "What's that?"

"Oh, sorry, it's something my mom always tells my dad. She got it from my grandad. Basically, it means she's not going to do every little menial task he requires of her." I laughed. "So hopefully, your brother isn't expecting me to completely run his life."

I studied Henry, trying to work up the courage to ask him some questions about his brother. I knew he was making fun of Wade, but ultimately Wade was still his brother, and that meant his loyalties would be to him and not to some random girl he'd only known for twenty minutes.

"Oh, Wade will definitely expect you to be his bootlicker." Henry turned onto a long winding road, and I looked out of the windows curiously. The street was lined with tall, mature trees, and I could see some cows and goats chewing on the grass in a field beyond. The sides of the field were covered in pink and purple wildflowers. I smiled as I sat back. Maybe it wouldn't be so bad to be out here. I loved the city, but sometimes it was overwhelming being surrounded by buildings, people, and constant traffic. There was no peace in the city. Everyone was always on the move. There was a constant buzzing that never stilled. Here, in Herne Hill Village, it seemed as if the only buzzing to worry about would be the bees.

"You're okay with that?" Henry looked at me with an expression of surprise on his face and I turned away from the scenery and looked at him.

"Sorry, I didn't hear what you said. Okay with what?"

"I said that Wade will expect you to be at his beck and call."

"I guess I'll just have to see." I shrugged nonchalantly. I wasn't going to get into a conversation with Henry about his brother before I'd even started. "Is there much to do in Herne Hill Village? Will I have access to a bike or a car or anything?"

"I don't really know what Wade will give you." He shook his head. "There's not much going on here. We have a couple of restaurants, a bakery, a bar." He laughed. "The usual for a small, popping village."

"That's a bit of an oxymoron." I grinned. "Small and popping."

"Herne Hill is quite the place to be." He made a sharp right and muttered under his breath. I looked ahead to see a herd of cows crossing the road. "Old man Sharpe just lets these things do what they want."

"Things? Or cows?"

"Oh, you'll see all his animals all over town." He shook his head. "Ridiculous."

"Are you from here then?" I looked at him curiously. Henry didn't strike me as a small-town man, but from the way he talked, he seemed familiar with Hern Hill Village and its inhabitants.

"Not really." He shook his head. "My parents divorced when I was three. My mom moved to Paris, and my dad moved here. Wade and I lived with my mom full time—well, she had custody of us. We went to boarding school in England. However, we spent every summer here with my dad. Then for college, Wade moved to Boston and I went to LA."

"And now you and Wade work together?" I asked, curious if I'd be seeing more of Henry. I snuck another glance at his profile. He was very handsome and he had a good sense of humor. It wouldn't be so bad if he was around.

"Not really." He laughed and then turned on the radio. I took that as my signal to stop asking questions and looked back out of the window. I wanted to call Lucy and tell her about Henry and this small town, but I would do it after I met Wade. As soon as I thought about him, my heart started racing again. I was much more nervous than I'd thought I'd be, starting this new job. Would he be like Henry? Was Wade a sheep in wolf's clothing? Or was he the kind to look all sweet and innocent on the outside, but on the inside he was all angry and tormented? If his phone conversations were anything to go by, he was going to be one interesting and annoying man.

About an hour later, we pulled into a long driveway. My jaw dropped as I saw the mansion that sat at the end of the driveway, surrounded by freshly mowed green lawns and perfectly trimmed bushes.

"We're here!" Henry announced. He hadn't been lying when he'd said Wade lived in an estate.

"Wow!" I couldn't believe how large the house and grounds were. "Wade has no help?"

"Well ..." Henry looked at me for a few seconds and shook his head slightly. "No inside help. No housekeeper, no cook, no cleaner, no butler, no one." He bit down on his lower lip. "He does have a man come in once a week to tend to the gardens, though."

"So who cleans the house?" I asked, gawking at the building as we stopped behind another car. "Please do not tell me that this will be part of my job. There's no way."

"I can't say." He shrugged. "I don't know what my brother has planned."

"Do you live here as well?"

"Oh, no."

"I meant, are you staying here while you're in town?"

"No." He shook his head. "Wade and I don't see eye to eye on many things. I'm staying in a cottage on the edge of the grounds."

"Wow, how big is the property?"

"We have ten acres here. There's a creek southwest of here, near the woods. My dad built a small cottage back there for gutting."

"Gutting?"

"He liked to hunt. We have deer and wild rabbits back there in the woods. He preferred to skin them and clean them near the woods instead of here."

"Oh." I felt a bit queasy. "Do you hunt?"

"Not me. It's a barbaric sport." He paused. "But Wade does."

"Hmm." My lips thinned. I was liking Wade less and less, and I hadn't even met him yet. I looked towards the front door, expecting to see him open it to greet me, but it remained closed. "Is he here?"

"Yes, I suppose he's still in his meeting or something." He shrugged and we got out of the car. "Let me grab your suitcase, and we can head inside."

"Okay." I was disappointed that Wade hadn't come to meet me, but what did I expect? I had already thought he was a bit of a pompous jerk. Now it was confirmed.

"I'm not sure what room he has you in, so I can't take you to your bedroom, but I can show you around the kitchen, the living area, the pool, and stuff."

"Thanks. That would be great."

I walked over to a rose shrub at the front of the house. The flowers were pale pink and the vine was crawling along the facade of the house, framing one of the windows. I peeked inside the window and saw what appeared to be a formal living room. I stepped back as Henry walked past me and towards the front door. He looked back at me, and I hurried to join him as he pulled out a key and unlocked the large black door. He held it open for me and I walked into a spacious foyer with vaulted ceilings. Immediately to the right, there was a large ornate mirror with a gold frame hanging on the wall over a mahogany wood console that featured an array of small vases. To the right of me hung a bear's head prominently attached to the wall, its eyes vacant and its teeth ferocious. I shivered at the sight of it and wondered why it was there. It didn't seem to fit the setting, but I didn't ask Henry any questions. I wasn't sure if I wanted to know.

"Wade, buddy ol' boy, we're here!" Henry dropped my suitcase on the ground as he called out into the house. He turned to me and winked as he let out a loud cat call whistle. I stood there, slightly uncomfortable, as we waited.

"I thought you were going to show me around."

"I am, but I wanted to let Wade know we were here. He's most probably in the office or something on a call." He shrugged. "Want to have a look around?"

"Sure." I held my handbag close to me and nodded. A chill filled me as we made our way down the long corridor. The hallway was eerily spooky asides from the sounds of our footsteps as we walked across the light gray and white marble. I followed behind Henry and tried not to gawk as we walked down a hallway filled with paintings that appeared to be original Caravaggios, Monets, and Rembrandts. I didn't have the best eye, but I'd spent enough time in art history classes and museums in Europe to recognize the masters when I saw them.

"I'll take you to the back first and then we can come back inside and explore the house." Henry offered me an impish smile as he turned to look back at me. "And maybe my brother will make an appearance."

"Sounds good."

We walked through a large kitchen towards some French doors, which led to a back patio that highlighted the vast grounds behind us. Henry made a sharp left, and we headed towards what appeared to be the pool area.

"No way." Henry stopped still at the side of a lounge chair. I followed his gaze to see what he was looking at and froze as I watched a long, lean golden body slicing through the water doing the front crawl. My eyes were drawn to the toned muscular arms as they sliced fluidly through the water. It was almost like watching a dolphin.

"Wade!" Henry walked towards the pool. "Yo, dipshit!" He grabbed a white towel that was placed on the lounge chair and threw it at the figure in the pool as it passed us again. The swimmer stopped and stood up straight. He had goggles on, so I couldn't see his face properly, but from what I could see of his chest, he was built like a sleek, well-oiled sports car. I swallowed hard as he took off his goggles and ran his hands through his slick wet hair.

"Henry." That familiar voice, condescending yet sexy, floated through the air. I hated that butterflies soared through my stomach at the sound of it. His eyes then turned to me and I watched as he looked me over, his expression giving nothing away as he stared at me. "And you must be Savannah."

"Yes." I bit down on my lower lip to stop myself from continuing, but I couldn't help myself. "And you must be *The Wade Hart*." My upper lip curled and I knew I sounded like a bitch, but really? He was swimming while his brother was picking me up at the train station and showing me around his house.

"I am." His lips twitched.

Wade swam over to us then put his hands on the side of the pool and hoisted his body up before I could even blink.

He shook the water from his hair and out of his eyes with a quick flick of his head. I gasped as hundreds of droplets splashed me. Instead of apologizing, he offered me a sardonic look and then took a step closer to me.

He was a lot taller than I'd thought when I'd seen him in the pool. Not that I'd thought he was short, but I'd imagined he'd be about Henry's height, and Henry was about six feet. Wade, however, towered over both me and his brother. He appeared to be about six foot four and all muscle. Water droplets rolled down his chest, and I stared at his toned abs and pecs a moment longer than was polite before looking back up into his face.

If I'd thought Henry was handsome, I was blown away by Wade. He was absolutely, spine-tinglingly *gorgeous*. His dark hair was slick and black, his eyes a light, teasing aqua-green that pierced my soul, his lips were juicy and pink against his dark olive complexion, and he had a hint of stubble on his cheeks and chin that I wanted to run my fingers across. My heart did a hundred flip flops as I stood there, and I prayed to God that he couldn't see in my face how attractive I found him.

"So, you made it on time." He smiled at me, though it wasn't a warm, happy smile. More of a self-congratulatory grin that irritated me as soon as I saw it.

"Obviously." I could see Henry staring at us, an amused expression on his face, but I just couldn't stop my sarcastic retorts.

"I take it you found the money deposited into your account this morning?"

"I wouldn't be here if I hadn't."

"Well, aren't you just a sweet pleasant surprise?" He tilted his head to the side and then looked at his brother. "You just can't get good help these days." My back stiffened at his comment but I didn't deign to respond.

"Well, I think that Savannah is lovely." Henry took a step closer to me. "Not only is she beautiful, but she's smart and witty as well." He winked at me and I smiled warmly at him, appreciating his comment and the fact that he'd called me beautiful.

"She's not going to sleep with you just because you complimented her." Wade laughed as his eyes flew back to my face and narrowed. The smile left my lips, and I glared at him. "Or maybe you would." He shrugged and took a step back. "Doesn't really matter, you won't have the opportunity. You'll be too busy working."

"Yes sir, no sir, two bags full, sir, anything you need right now, sir?" I did a little courtesy and plastered a fake smile on my face. Henry laughed as Wade raised an eyebrow at me.

"I'm taking it you're not an actress. Your Yorkshire accent needs a lot of work."

"It wasn't a Yorkshire accent."

"Exactly, that's what I just said." He grinned at me. "It wasn't anywhere close." Before I could respond again, he turned around and dove back into the pool and started doing laps. I stared at him for a few seconds before turning to Henry. I could feel my chest rising as I controlled my anger.

"Your brother is an asshole." I resisted my first urge, which was to jump into the pool and splash him. I didn't even want to acknowledge my second urge because it made even the inner me blush.

"He is." Henry laughed. "I'm surprised you took this job."

"You and me both." I shook my head. "Maybe this isn't worth it."

"I can drive you back to the train station if you want to leave?" He looked almost hopeful, and I wondered if he wanted me to quit. "I mean if you need a ride." He looked away. "It's up to you."

"No, it's fine for now. I'll see how the work goes. I'm guessing the meetings he needed me for so urgently this morning no longer exist?" I shook my head and let out a sigh. "I'm glad I woke up at five a.m. to get here on time."

"I can see how that could be annoying." Henry pulled out his phone. "Look, I really hate to do this, especially considering how your first meeting with Wade just went, but I actually have to go. I just got a text about something important and I need to head to my cottage and take care of some business. I hope you don't mind?"

"No, that's fine. Thanks for picking me up."

"You're welcome, Savannah. Don't let my brother get to you. Feel free to put him in his place if you need to. He's more bark than bite."

"Okay, I'll remember that. Thanks." I nodded at him and then walked to the lounger to sit down as Henry walked away. I sat there watching Wade continue to swim, and I could feel myself growing angrier and angrier as the time went on. How long was he going to keep swimming? Finally, I grabbed my phone from my bag so that I could text Lucy.

Savannah: Lucy, I'm here!

Lucy: How is it? Amazing?

Savannah: Do you think there is any chance it's amazing?

Lucy: Wow, that bad?

Savannah: Worse, Wade Hart is a bigger jerk than I even thought he was going to be.

Lucy: Oh wow, what happened?

Savannah: Well, remember how he said he wanted me to—

"It must be nice to have a job where you get paid for texting." Wade's deep voice almost made me jump as his shadow crossed my screen. I jumped up and rolled my eyes.

"Well, it's not as if I have anything to do."

"You saw the kitchen, didn't you?"

"Yeah, so?"

"Didn't I tell you I wanted you to prepare my meals?"

"You said lunch and dinner. You said you'd take care of breakfast yourself."

"Oh, did I?" He chuckled. "Well, change of plans. You're in charge of that as well."

"Okay." My lips thinned. I would not argue with him. I would not let him get the better of me. "Do you want me to make it now?"

"No," He shook his head and I stared into his sparkling eyes. "I think you'd poison me if I asked you to cook me breakfast now."

"Well, you might be an asshole, but at least you're astute."

"You think I'm an asshole?" He smirked. "I'm your boss. Do you really think that's an appropriate thing to say?"

"Do you really think you've been appropriate?"

"How have I been inappropriate?" He cocked his head to the side and counted on his fingers. "I hired you for a job, I paid you a hundred grand in advance, I had my brother pick you up at the train station, I'm taking my morning swim as I do every morning." He paused and his voice grew huskier and lower. "Tell me Savannah, how exactly have I been inappropriate?"

He knew he had me. What could I say? That he'd made me get here early to work when it obviously hadn't been needed? Was that really something to complain about? I couldn't tell him that his tone and look simply irritated me. I was in the wrong. I'd been rude, blatantly rude. Shit, most people would have fired me already for my comments.

"Maybe you haven't," I said finally, hating myself for my words as soon as I saw the wide satisfied smile on his face.

"That's more like it." He looked me up and down again,

slowly. "You're pretty." He stared in my eyes, a curious look on his face. "You could have sent a photo."

"I didn't want to send a photo." I stared at him obstinately. "That was a rude request."

"Yes, I can see how it might have been a bit inappropriate."

"Just a bit?" I shook my head. "Maybe a lot."

"Well, I can tell you that I'm not disappointed."

"Okay, and?"

"I just thought you'd like to know that I think you're passable."

"Passable? Just now I was pretty, and your brother called me beautiful, but now I'm only passable?"

"Do you have a thing for Henry?" he blurted out, his gaze intense on my face.

"What are you talking about? I just met him." I stared pointedly at his dripping body. "Are you going to grab a towel? Are we going to start working?"

"You're awfully bold and bossy for someone on their first day." He raised an eyebrow. "And for someone who obviously needs the money."

"Look, I don't need the money that badly," I lied. "If this working relationship is going to continue like this, then maybe it's best if I just leave now."

"Do you want to leave?" His question lingered in the air for a few seconds and we just stared at each other. As I gazed at him, I realized I didn't want to leave and it had nothing to do with the money.

"Are we going to work? Maybe if I find out more about my tasks, I will be able to decide. Also, will I have access to a car? I don't want to be stuck here all day and night at your mercy."

"Can you drive?" His lips twitched.

"Yes."

"Then you will have access to a car. Don't get too excited, though. You won't have that much free time."

"Legally, you need to give me breaks and days off."

"You talk like a lawyer."

"I'm not a lawyer."

"That I already know, Ms. Savannah Carter." He grabbed another towel from the lounge chair and wrapped it around his shoulders. "Come, let's go inside. I'll show you to your room while I change, and to make things up to you, how's about I make you breakfast?"

"You're not going to poison me, are you?" I offered him a small smile and he laughed, a deep warm sound filling the air as we made our way into the house.

"You wouldn't know until it was too late if I did." He winked then looked away. I shivered. Wade Hart was going to be trouble. I could feel it, but I didn't care. I'd never had a proper adventure in my life, and I was ready to start now.

CHAPTER 6

"Did my brother show you around the house yet?"

"No, he hasn't shown me anything aside from the pool area."

"Figures." Wade muttered something under his breath and then walked over to the fridge. "Would you like a green juice?"

"No thanks." I watched as he opened the door and took out a little plastic bottle. He opened it and chugged it down and then placed the container on the countertop.

"I like green juice every morning before my workout." He strummed his fingers against the countertop and continued. "Celery, cucumber, cilantro, apples, and some ginger. Fresh."

"Okay, and why are you telling me this information?"

"You'll be making it. You'll go to the Farmers Market in the village every Wednesday and Sunday to get the ingredients. I will join you on Sundays."

"Why don't I go on Wednesday and you go on Sundays? Why do I have to go both days?"

"You'll create menus for the week by Monday so that I

can approve them. And you'll do the shopping for them on the same days you go to the market." He ignored my question and I held in a rude comment. "Understand?"

I stared back at him, not saying anything. If he could ignore my questions, I could certainly ignore his questions.

"I said, understand?"

"And I said, why do we both—"

"I'm the boss here, Savannah. You speak when you're spoken to and you answer my questions, not the other way around. You don't get to make the rules."

"Excuse me, who the hell do you think you are, my dad?" My voice rose. "I am your employee, not your slave. I can speak whenever the hell I like and I can ask whatever questions I want. You're not some dictator in some small country who can force me to act a certain way."

"I don't think anyone could force you to do anything." He turned around. "Where are your bags? Let's take them to your room."

"So you're just not going to answer my questions?" I ran after him. "Really?" I reached out and touched his arm, and a sudden jolt of electricity shocked me. He stopped walking and turned to me, a sudden light in his eyes that hadn't existed before.

"If you wanted to touch me, you just had to ask."

"I didn't want to touch you, I was just ..." My voice trailed off as my face heated. *Fuck it, fuck it, why was he looking at me like that?* Like he could see into my mind and soul. Like he knew that my fingers were still tingling from the brief feel of his warm, silky skin and the taut muscles beneath. I wondered just how strong he was … and what he could do with me if he had me in the bedroom.

Get your mind out of the gutter, Savannah!

Oh God, why was I thinking about him in the bedroom? My eyes flew to his chest and his nipples. My throat felt dry as my eyes continued downwards. His stomach was tight and ripped, and yet my eyes kept going. Before I'd been too fired up to notice that he was wearing a speedo. A very tight speedo. *Oh shit!* I swallowed hard as my eyes rested on his manhood. Was he hard or soft right now? He was huge. If he was hard, why was he hard and if he was soft, how much bigger would he be when he was hard?

While I wasn't that experienced, I had seen a cock before, and it hadn't inspired much interest or desire. But now, standing next to this gorgeous, infuriating man, I was curious. What would he look like completely naked?

"Like what you see?" he said quietly.

My eyes flew back to his face. Oh shit, had he caught me checking out his package?

"I haven't seen my room yet, so I don't know if I will like it." I coughed and then hurried past him to the foyer, so that I could grab my suitcase. What the hell was I thinking, checking him out like that? Right in front of him? Had I lost my mind?

"I'll get that for you." He brushed past me and grabbed the handle of my suitcase.

"I'm surprised you don't want me to carry it myself."

"I'm the consummate gentleman, Savannah. You may not realize that yet, but truly, you won't find a better guy than me." He said the words so seriously that I couldn't stop myself from laughing. I was laughing so hard that tears were falling out of my eyes. "What's so funny?" He looked amused as he watched me.

"The fact that you think you're a gentleman? On what planet?" I giggled as the words tripped out. "You're the furthest thing from a gentleman that I've ever seen!"

"Really?"

"Yes, really." I nodded, catching my breath as we continued walking.

"I suppose your boyfriend is a real gentleman, huh?" He studied my face, and I knew that was his way of asking if I was dating someone. Not that I was going to tell him.

"Yes, yes, he is."

"He's so caring that he let you just take this job in the country with a handsome older man."

"He didn't *let* me do anything. I do what I want."

"A regular twenty-first century woman, aren't you?"

"What's that supposed to mean? I'm sure your girlfriend loves how rude you are."

"I don't have a girlfriend." He stopped outside of a door and pushed it open. "I'm single, free, and unattached."

"She dumped you, huh?" I murmured as we walked into the room, then I gasped at the beauty before me, forgetting about our little spat. The room was larger than my entire apartment in New York City. Immediately in front of me was a sitting area, with a comfortable couch, table and TV; to the right of the room was a four-poster king-sized bed with huge, fluffy pillows. To the left of the bed there was a door, and I walked through it into an enormous en suite, which had a walk-in shower, a huge clawfoot tub, and a wide full-length mirror. I walked back out of the bathroom and saw that Wade was standing next to the bed, my case on the ground next to him.

"Does it please your ladyship?" He bowed his head. "If you don't like it, then there are four other suites for you to choose from."

"I love it," I said breathlessly. "It's amazing." I forgot that I was mad at him. Forgot that he was an annoying asshole. I looked into his face with a bright smile. "It's really lovely, and that smell! It smells like fresh flowers."

"That's because they are." He nodded to a chest of drawers on the other side of the room. On top of the chest sat a tall vase full of pink, purple, yellow and white flowers.

"I picked them for you this morning. I wanted to make the room welcoming."

"Really?" I was taken aback by the kind gesture. "Thank you."

"Yes. And I will give you a ten-thousand-dollar budget to change anything in the room that you want."

"No way, wow!"

"I want this to feel like your home. Is there anything that you can think that you want?"

"Maybe a writing desk?"

"You're a writer?"

"Well, not really. I've never had anything published or anything."

"But you write?"

"Yes."

"What do you write?" He actually looked interested in what I had to say, and I felt myself warming to him. Maybe he wasn't as bad as I'd thought. Maybe he just had an off-putting exterior. For all I knew, he didn't realize just how he was coming off.

"Poetry."

"Poetry, eh?" He nodded. "Epic stuff?"

"Not really. More short and punchy verses. I like to participate in poetry slams."

He winced. "Oh, not that airy-fairy stuff?"

"What's airy-fairy about poetry slams?" I glared at him, my back stiffening again. Maybe I hadn't been wrong about him after all.

"Are your poems about your emotions and feelings or more epic tales?"

"Is there anything wrong with poems about emotions?"

"Nothing at all." He shook his head. "Maybe we can go into town later this afternoon to look for a writing desk for you."

"We don't have to do that." I shook my head. "Save your money. It might not work out."

"What might not work out?"

"This whole situation." I waved my arms around. "I just don't know if this is really going to work."

"What if I offered you another $50,000 to convince you to stay for a month?" He stared directly into my eyes. "And if in thirty days, you still want to leave, you can keep the entire $150,000 and move on with your life."

"That seems crazy." I shook my head. "I can't just take your money."

"You wouldn't just be taking my money. You'd be working for me." He shrugged. "I'd expect you to do all your duties. And you can't quit."

"Hmmm …" I considered my options. How hard could it be? Thirty days and then I could leave. "I'm not sure."

"Are you that afraid of hard work?"

"Of course not."

"Then we have a deal?"

"Fine." I held my hand out. "We have a deal."

"Good." He smiled. "I had a feeling you'd say yes." He looked around the room and smiled. "Now, I'm going to go and have a shower. Meet me in the kitchen in fifteen minutes."

"Okay."

"Just okay?"

"What else am I supposed to say?"

"I thought you'd add a *sir* or something." He grinned and then turned around and headed out of the room before I could think of a response. The door slammed behind him.

I stood there just breathing and taking everything in. It was official, I was crazy. The mad house could come and pick me up at any time because I had officially lost it. What the hell had I just agreed to? I walked over to the bed, sat down, leaned back into the stack of pillows, and closed my eyes.

Immediately Wade's face came to mind, and I allowed myself to envision his dazzling green eyes and charming smile as I lay there. I wondered why he didn't have a girlfriend, and I wondered if he would ask to meet my imaginary boyfriend. I wasn't quite sure why I'd lied. Actually, that was untrue; I knew exactly why I'd lied. I could feel a chemistry between Wade and me, and I didn't want either one of us to act on it. If he thought I had a boyfriend, he wouldn't try to seduce me or expect that anything would happen with us.

Not that I thought *he* would be interested in *me*. The lie was like an insurance policy. I didn't want us to have anything other than a professional relationship … although I had to admit we might have already crossed that line.

CHAPTER 7

"I hope you like scrambled eggs and bacon." A dressed Wade greeted me as I made my way into the kitchen. "Would you like toast or a bagel?"

"Toast, please." I headed towards the island. "Is there anything I can do to help?"

"Grab the bag of bread and put four slices in the toaster." He gestured to the countertop behind him. "You'll find the butter and jam in the fridge."

"Okay." I pulled four slices of bread out of the bag and placing them into the stainless-steel toaster. I stared down at it, waiting for the bread to turn from white to a golden brown, instead of turning around to study Wade, which is what I really wanted to do.

"Do you want any fruit?"

I jumped at the sound of Wade's voice in my ear. He'd walked over to me without me even noticing, quiet as a mouse.

He grinned as if he knew what I was thinking. "I hunt, I'm used to moving without anyone realizing. I take it you don't like hunting."

I frowned. "Are you a mind reader?"

"No, but your face is very expressive."

"I didn't realize." I looked down into the toaster, trying to tell what color the bread was. I couldn't tell, so I pressed the button for the toast to pop up. It was still white and soft, so I pressed the button down again for it to toast some more.

"Are you scared to look at me?"

"Of course not," I replied, but my heart was racing as I looked back up at him. There was a teasing light in his brooding, beautiful eyes, and I wondered what he was thinking.

"So, it looked like you and Henry got on well?"

"Yeah, he seemed like a nice guy." I stopped myself from adding *unlike you*.

"I bet you wish he was your boss, huh?"

"Well, I wouldn't say that ..."

He burst out laughing and I could see his eyes surveying my face. "You wouldn't say it, but you're thinking it, huh?

I shrugged my response, and he grinned at my lack of reply.

"You don't look like a girl that would be into standup poetry."

"First off, I'm not a girl, and secondly, what is a woman who's a poet supposed look like?"

"I thought you'd have on tie dye t-shirts and black jeans."

"Are you still in the 90's?" I shook my head. "What a stereotype!"

"So, you studied English? At Columbia?"

"Yes."

"Any books you want to recommend?"

"Not really."

"I'm trying to get to know you, and you're making this really hard."

"Am I?" I smiled wickedly at him and then blushed. Where the hell had that come from?

"Yes, yes, you are." He looked like he wanted to say something else. I could tell from his expression that he was unsure whether I was being deliberately naughty or not and I liked it that way. Let him guess if I was dropping sexual innuendos on his doorstep. He unnerved me, and I didn't mind thinking I unnerved him slightly as well. Even if it was only in my head. "Well, if you're finished eating and you don't want to answer any of my questions, why don't you wash up these dishes and then meet me in my office in about fifteen minutes and we can start working."

"You want me to wash up the dishes?"

"Do you have a problem with that?"

"Don't you have a dishwasher?"

"Yes."

"So why do I have to ..." My voice trailed off as he stood up and walked out of the room.

"Fifteen minutes, Savannah."

"Fifteen minutes, Savannah," I muttered under my breath. "Maybe actually answer a question, asshole."

"My name's Wade, not asshole." He stopped dead in the hallway and looked back at me. "Unless you know something I don't know?" He laughed and my face burned as he turned back around. Who was he, Batman? How had he heard me? Was I really that loud?

I glanced at the dirty dishes on the table and sighed. How was this my life? I didn't even enjoy doing the dishes at home. I grabbed the plates and headed over to the sink. All I could think about was buying a calendar so I could count down the days until I could leave this job and move on with my life. Once I was debt-free, I'd be able to do whatever I wanted. I would just have to remind myself of that every time Wade said or did something that got on my nerves.

✦

"**H**ave a seat, Savannah." Wade waved me into his office as I hovered timidly in the door opening. "I'm on hold on a conference call, but I'll be off in a few minutes, and then we can get started."

"Okay."

I walked into his office and looked around quickly before taking a seat in a dark mahogany wooden chair that had been upholstered in a deep red leather. I sat down, pleasantly surprised at how comfortable the chair was. I clutched the pen that was in hand and clicked it on and scribbled Day One and the date on top of the yellow legal pad that I'd brought with me then sat back. Wade was watching me with an amused expression on his face. "What exactly will I be doing today?" I asked, wanting him to stop looking at me like the cat that had got the cream.

"Today we'll be on a call with the heads of a small village in Uganda and some members of their parliament. We're building some sustainable farms and wells."

"The government is building them or you're building them?"

"I am building them. Well, providing the resources. Local workers will be trained and will run the farms." He picked up a pen and scribbled something on a notepad in front of him. "Have you ever been to Uganda?"

"No."

"Have you ever been to Africa?"

"No." I offered him a rueful smile. "I've always wanted to go to Kenya or South Africa to go on a safari. And also to Egypt to see the pyramids." I shrugged. "One day, when I have some money, I will make it."

"Yes, you will." He nodded. "You will notice that North Africa is very different to sub-Saharan Africa."

"Have you been, then?"

"Yes, I have worked in conjunction with the World Bank and some other organizations, and I've travelled quite extensively in the continent." He nodded. "Today I need you to take notes on the conversation. I take it you know shorthand?"

"Not really."

"Well, can you type fast?" He looked at my lap. "Do you have a laptop?"

"I didn't bring it with me." I bit down on my lower lip. "It's the same laptop I've had since high school, and it's really slow. I need a new one ... Not that I'm asking you for a new one or anything," I added on quickly, lest he think that I was begging for something else.

He chuckled and sat back. "I think I've paid you enough to afford a new one, but don't worry. I have a laptop you can use for work business."

"What about non-work business?"

"You can send personal emails, yes, but I wouldn't use it to surf porn sites, if I were you. I have access to every website that is visited, and I don't want to be privy to the fact that my new assistant has a penchant for stepfather porn or threesomes."

"What?" My jaw dropped and my face reddened. "What are you talking about?"

"I'm just saying if you visit porn websites to pleasure yourself at night, I will know. And I'm not sure you want me knowing what your sexual fantasies are."

"I don't visit porn websites, Mr. Hart, and I don't appreciate your comments. In fact, I would go so far as to say that you've crossed the line again."

"Again?" His lips twisted and I could see his perfect white teeth as he grinned. "Are you saying that I've crossed the line more than once?"

"It's not appropriate to talk to me about porn websites."

"I'm not talking about porn websites. You're the one that asked me if you could use the laptop for personal reasons."

"I meant sending emails and maybe checking my social media accounts. Nothing other than that. I don't even watch porn."

"You don't watch porn?" He leaned forward. "Really?"

"Really!" I blushed. "Not that it's any of your business."

"So, when you masturbate you have images in your mind, then?"

"Excuse me!" I jumped up. "I'm not having this conversation with you!" I made my way to the door and I could feel my chest rising. "If you think that you can just say whatever you want to me, then I'll have you know that —" I stopped talking as Wade jumped up from behind his desk and walked over to me. "What are you doing?" I licked my lips nervously as he stopped right in front of me, his green eyes twinkling.

"I wanted to apologize to you," he said smoothly as he touched my arm. "I can see that I've upset you, and that wasn't my intention. I just wanted to make it clear that while you're welcome to pleasure yourself in any way you want, maybe it would be best if—"

"Just stop." I interrupted him. "Stop talking about me in that way. Do you really think that's appropriate?"

"Maybe not." He stared at my lips. "But this entire situation is just a little different to the norm, isn't it?"

"Yes, but that's on you, not on me." A thought struck me. "Oh God, this job isn't some sort of sex thing, is it? Did you hire me to be your sex toy or plaything or something?"

"My sex toy?" He chuckled. "How would you be my sex toy?"

"I don't know, but if you think I'm here to be your sexual playmate, you're in for a huge surprise because I am not a whore, or a slut, or a hooker." I was almost shouting now. "I came here for a professional job. And I'm here to work as your assistant, not to fulfil any of your sick fantasies!"

"Who said my fantasies are sick?" He winked at me. "Or are you a mind reader?"

"I'm not a mind reader, but I'm pretty sure I could guess."

"You have a pretty face," he said abruptly. "You could have sent me a photo." He looked me over. "You don't look much like a dog at all."

"And you, sir, don't look like a gentleman."

"Did I say I was one?"

"Are we going to work or what?" I walked back to the chair so that I could get away from him. "And where's this uniform that you said you wanted me to wear?"

"I'll have the uniform ready for you tomorrow." He walked back to his side of the desk and sat down. "Looks like these people are never going to get back to me." He frowned and then pressed a button on the conference phone on his desk. "You can call them back for me later this afternoon, introduce yourself as my assistant, and let them know you need the numbers for the graphite project."

"Okay." I quickly added that to my notepad and watched as he lightly tapped some numbers into the phone and pressed the speaker button. His fingers were long, with neatly trimmed nails, and I wondered what they would feel like against my skin. The phone rang three times, and then a very polite woman answered the phone.

"You've reached the office of Minister Akello, this is Dembe speaking. How may I help you today?"

"Dembe, good to speak to you, this is Wade Hart on the phone, calling from New York. I have a call with Minister Akello and some local politicians in Gayaza. Can you put me through?"

"Oh, nice to speak to you, Mr. Hart. Would you mind

holding one minute? I will tell Minister Akello you're on the line."

'That's perfect, have a great day, Dembe," Wade said politely, and I could feel the shock spreading through me. So he could be a normal respectful human being, then?

"Close your mouth, Savannah, you don't want to catch any flies—or maybe you do?"

"Are you going to give me the laptop to take these notes?" I said pointedly, ignoring his comment. I wondered if our working relationship was going to continue this way, with each of us only answering half of the other's questions. I'd never met anyone like him before. The men I'd known could only be classified as boys when compared to him. They even looked like boys in comparison to him. I could still picture his half naked body by the pool, and the way the water had glistened as it ran down his chest.

"Yes, I suppose I should get that for you now before the call starts." He stood up and walked past me and to a file cabinet in the corner of the room. He opened the bottom cabinet and pulled out what appeared to be a brand new MacBook Pro. He handed it to me and I opened the screen. I pressed the power button as he went back to his seat and then he grinned at me.

"The password to get in is The Wade Hart."

"You've got to be joking me." I couldn't believe it, but I quickly found out that he wasn't joking as I typed in the letters and gained access to the desktop. "You really are full of yourself, aren't you?"

"No, but I like that you think I am."

"You really like that I think that?"

"Would I have said I did if I didn't?"

"Are you always this difficult?"

"Are you?"

I just glared at him and sighed. What the hell was his

problem? And why was he smirking at me as if he'd found our whole exchange extremely funny? Nothing about this situation was funny. Absolutely nothing at all. "I'm sorry, but when I went to school, we were taught to respect our elders, I will watch what I say from here on out." I smiled sweetly.

"You consider me your elder?" He raised an eyebrow. "I'm thirty."

"And your point is?"

"No point." He shook his head. "You don't have to cook dinner tonight. Not sure if I already mentioned that or not. But we will grab a pizza."

"Okay, cool."

"Ham and pineapple."

"Gross." I wrinkled my nose. "I'm not okay with pineapple on a pizza."

"You know what they say about pineapple on a pizza right?"

"No, what?"

"If you don't know, I can't tell you." He winked and I was about to press him to tell me what he was insinuating, when his expression suddenly changed. "Okay, my call is about to start. Open up a Word doc and get ready. You might not understand everything, but type out everything that you can."

"Yes, sir."

"You sure do act like someone that doesn't want to keep her job."

"And you act like someone that doesn't want to keep his assistant."

"Touché." He cocked his head to the side and then laughed. "You do know that I can easily get another assistant, right? You might find it a lot harder to find a new job."

"Why are you saying I'm not a good assistant?"

"I'm not saying you're bad, but I'm definitely not saying you're good, either."

I had to resist the urge to slap the smirk off of his face. He sure wouldn't be laughing then. But then neither would I. He would surely fire me if I slapped him, and for all I knew he would call the cops and I'd also taken to jail. I certainly didn't need to get a criminal record just to make a point.

There was a beep on the line, and Wade pressed a finger to his lips. "Okay, shh, the call is starting."

"Hello, Mr. Hart, Minister Akello here along with Minister Opio and Minister Adong."

"Hello, Ministers Akello, Opio and Adong, this is Wade Hart on the line. I also have my assistant Savannah Carter listening in as she will be taking notes for me, I hope that's okay."

"Of course, Mr. Hart. Nice to meet you, Mrs. Carter."

"Hi, it's miss and nice to meet you as well," I said quickly. Wade was still smirking.

"So, Mr. Hart, we understand that you have taken our needs into consideration and come up with a plan?"

"Yes," The tone of Wade's voice changed, and I listened in awe as he began talking about investing in the farming industry in Uganda and helping to set up distribution centers for export. I typed as quickly as possible, but I couldn't help glancing at him in amazement once in a while as he discussed investing millions into training and infrastructure, all from his own bank account. I wondered why he was doing it. Granted, it was a worthwhile and needed project, but from the looks of him, Wade had no connection to Africa from what I could see. Why would he want to invest so much money into a continent and country that was so far removed from his life?

"Well, Mr. Hart, that all sounds very good, but what guarantee do we have that the equipment you bring into the country will last? And also, we will need to train up our farmers and engineers on how to fix these new products. Money will also be needed for education. Our people know their current systems and current processes. We don't want to fix something that is already working."

"I respectfully disagree with you, Minister Akello. The number of people in poverty in those regions shows us that the current systems aren't working. You also stated on our last call that you rely far too much on imports when you have the capacity and workforce to manufacture a lot more domestically."

"That is true." Minister Akello paused. "You give me a lot to think about, Mr. Hart. The other ministers and I will discuss your proposal, and then we will reconvene next week with any questions."

"That sounds perfect. Have a great evening, Minister Akello."

"You too, Wade. Savannah, do not let him work you too hard." The minister chuckled and then hung up.

I stared at Wade, my stomach growling as I realized we'd been on the call for three hours. I finished typing up the last sentence, hit save, and then looked up at him.

"How would you like me to send you the notes I just typed up?" I asked him as he furiously scribbled something on a notepad. His face looked serious, and I realized that he wasn't paying any attention to me. I watched as he stood up and quickly grabbed a file from the shelf next to his desk. He opened it up and pulled out some papers, muttering under his breath. I stared at him as he worked. I wasn't hating it. In fact, I was a little impressed and a lot hot. He might be conceited and full of himself, but he wasn't just a self-obsessed prick. He was a businessman who seemed to care about more than just maximizing profits. "Wade?"

"Sorry, what did you say?" He looked up at me, a pen in his mouth and a slight frown on his forehead.

"I was just asking if you'd like me to email you the file? I can put it directly in the email or send as an attachment or upload to Dropbox ..." My voice drifted off as he stared at me with a small smile. The look on his face disconcerted me. He looked amused, and I had no idea why.

"You can email them for now. As an attachment." He paused as the phone on his desk started ringing. He looked at it and frowned. "Answer that, please, and let them know I'm not available."

"Uhm, okay?" I leaned over and picked up the phone. "This is Wade Hart's office, Savannah speaking. How may I help you?"

"Savannah who?" An airy female voice inquired.

"Savannah Carter?"

"And who are you, Savannah Carter?" The light voice was questioning and not as sweet.

"I'm Wade Hart's assistant, can I help you?"

"This is Louisa, I need to speak to Wade."

"Sorry, Ms. Louisa, but—"

"It's not Ms. Louisa, but Mrs. Thiefton." She paused. "I want to speak to my son."

"Your son?" I couldn't keep the shock out of my voice as I responded to her comment. I'd thought Louisa was his girl-friend or some woman Wade was seeing. Her voice sounded so young. I looked over at Wade to see if he wanted to take the call after all, but the expression on his face had changed from amusement to hostility. He shook his head and waved his hand in front of his neck. "I'm sorry, Mrs. Hart, but Wade is not—"

"Are you an imbecile?" Her voice was sharp now.

"Sorry, what?"

"I told you my name is Mrs. Thiefton."

"Oh, I'm sorry, Mrs. Thiefton, but Wade is not—"

"Listen, girl, I know my son is there with you. There's no way he would let you in his office without him there, put him on the phone."

"Mr. Hart is not available. Can I take a message?"

"No."

And with that she hung up. I held the phone in my hand and looked over at Wade. "She didn't sound too pleased."

"She'll get over it."

"I don't think your mom likes me."

"Don't feel bad, she doesn't like anyone."

"Not even you?" I teased him.

"Barely." He grinned. "Which is a shocker, I'm sure. She loves Henry, though."

"Well, he's perfect, so I can see why."

"You want in my brother's pants badly, don't you?"

"More than I want in yours," I retorted before I could stop myself. I groaned inwardly. Why had I said that? I could see that I'd amused him by the way he stared at my lips and raised one single, questioning eyebrow "But no, I'm not interested in him at all." I stood up. "Are we done? I want to go over these notes and then email them to you. I'd prefer to do it in my own space."

"Running away from me? I'm not the big bad wolf, Savannah."

"I'm not quite convinced of that," I said with a quick lick of my lips. "I wouldn't exactly call you a little piggy."

"Yeah, there's nothing little about me." He winked, I blushed, and the room went quiet. It was an odd situation to be working for a man who both annoyed me and turned me on. Half the time I didn't know if he was actually flirting with me or if he was trying to get a rise out of me. "So, are you going to your room to finish typing up your notes or are you just going to sit there looking pretty and gaping at me?"

I gave him my haughtiest look. "Now I know why you had to offer so much money to get an assistant. Someone has to be a saint or really in need of the money to put up with your assholery."

"Is that a word, then?" He tilted his head to the side. "May I have the Oxford Dictionary definition?"

"No, you may not," I huffed and walked out of the room, ignoring the sound of his laughter as I went. Just when I was starting to think he was okay, he went and said something that made me dislike him all over again. I couldn't wait to get to my bedroom to type up my notes and call Lucy. I was going to need all the talking down she could give me because right now even the money wasn't making this job seem worth it.

❦

"So, this is Herne Hill Village. It's not much, but I like to think it's a little slice of heaven." Wade beamed with pride as we stopped outside of a small organic grocery store. "This is where you can do your shopping for the week. If there are any ingredients you need that they don't have, you just have to let them know and they can get it in for you."

"Okay." I nodded, hoping he wasn't expecting me to prepare gourmet meals. He hadn't said he required me to be a Michelin-starred chef, or and he'd never asked me what my cooking skills were like. I just hoped he liked a lot of scrambled eggs on toast.

"Is there anything you wanted to have a look at before we figured out your desk?"

"No, not really." I was a little overwhelmed and wanted to explore the village at a later date when I was by myself.

"Okay then, so I figured you could see if you like any of the desks in the store on the corner."

"But that's not a store …" I stared at the dark building with the shuttered windows.

"It's not a traditional store, no, but it is a carpenter's studio. Chuck makes pieces out of reclaimed wood. He can make you up a nice desk, you just need to let him know the style that you like."

"A custom desk? For me? Won't that take forever to make?"

"He can most probably have it done in a week. And I want you to have a desk you'll love. Especially seeing as you'll be sitting at it most of the day."

"Would it be possible to have it be a sitting/standing desk?" I asked shyly, feeling a bit embarrassed by asking for something special. "I have a cousin who is a chiropractor, and he always says that if you're going to be at a desk most of the day, at least try not to be sitting the whole time."

"A sitting/standing desk?" Wade looked thoughtful. "We can ask what Chuck can do to make that happen, but aren't you a bit young to be worried about sitting for too long? You literally just entered the workforce."

"That doesn't mean that I don't care about my health and my back." I shook my head. "Prevention is better than cure."

"I guess you don't want to create any issues for your back. You don't want it to be uncomfortable when you're lying on it …" He winked at me and I glared at him.

"What is that supposed to mean? What are you insinuating?"

"I'm not insinuating anything. Don't you lie on your back when you sleep?" He shrugged. "Forgive my assumption, maybe you're a side sleeper. I couldn't imagine you sleep on your stomach, though."

"And why is that?"

"It doesn't seem as though it would be comfortable." His eyes fell to my breasts, and I blushed. "But what do I know?"

"I sleep on my back," I said finally. "And I sleep just well, though sometimes I do like to change up my position."

"I'm glad to hear that. I'm pretty versatile as well." He grinned. "I actually like to be on my back as well. Nothing like someone on—" He held up his hand as I glared at him. "Okay, I'll stop, let's go and chat with Chuck and see what he can do."

"Fine." I pursed my lips and followed him across the road. We passed a pub called The Half Moon, and he turned to look at me.

"If we get done in time and you're willing, we can grab a drink in there. You can meet some of the locals."

"Some of the locals?" I raised an eyebrow. "This really is a small village, isn't it?"

"Do you not like small villages?"

"I can't say if I like or dislike them." I shrugged. "I'm from the suburbs and live in New York City. I like the hustle and bustle of living in a big place, where no one knows my name and I can be whoever I want."

"And here everyone knows your name." He smiled gently. "You can still be whoever you want, though. No one can stop you from that."

"I am who I want to be." I shrugged. "Well, I am who I can afford to be in this moment," I conceded.

"If money wasn't an issue, who would you be?" He looked at me as if he really wanted to know the answer.

"I'm not sure."

"A world-famous author?"

"I don't know." I shook my head. "I'd love to be an author, but it's more than that. I don't actually just like writing. It's too solitary for me. I want to be out in the world. I want to interact with people." I shrugged. "I would need more than to just know that people were reading my books. I want them to feel my books through me."

"And I suppose that's why you enjoy poetry and performing?"

"I think so. There's something so vulnerable about standing up and sharing something you wrote in front of people and seeing their faces and their eyes." We stopped outside the carpenter's building. "It's hard to explain, but it's powerful."

"I guess I should tell you they have an open mic night at the pub every week. I'm sure you could perform some of your poetry there. If you are finished with your work, of course," he added.

"Of course," I agreed, but he'd lit a little flame of excitement in me. Maybe I didn't have to give up everything that I loved just to make some money.

"Have you ever thought about acting?"

"Nah." I smiled wryly. "I'm not really a good actress." I laughed. "My face is overly expressive."

"Isn't that a good thing?"

"No." I shook my head. "A good actress is more subtle in her emotions, just like a good author is more subtle in their words. It's the whole show-don't-tell thing."

"So you're a better author than actor?"

"Not yet. Not really. But I'm trying. It's hard for me to not shove my emotions and feelings into someone's face."

"I can see that." He laughed. "You certainly don't hold back, but I like that. You're very honest. Most people aren't so honest."

"I don't know that it helps me." I shrugged. "But I feel like I need to lead my life as transparently as possible."

"And you live a life true to yourself?"

"I like to think so."

"Was taking this job true to yourself?" His eyes narrowed

as he studied my face. Looking into his eyes, I felt like he was trying to read my soul. It made me feel uncomfortable and I wondered why I had opened up to him so easily. I couldn't stand the guy, yet there was something in his aura that attracted me to him. And it wasn't just his good looks. It was more than that.

Granted, I wanted to rip his shirt off and touch his chest and kiss his lips and pull his hair. I wanted to feel his teeth nipping on my breasts and his hands on my ass—

Shit! I blushed as dirty thoughts flooded through me. Was I that desperate for a man that I was standing here in the middle of the street fantasizing about my new boss?

"You look puzzled. Are you okay, Savannah?" Wade's voice was teasing.

I blinked and ran my fingers through my hair before tugging it behind my ear. "Yeah, sorry, uhm. Our conversation went a lot deeper than I was expecting."

"I hear that a lot." He grinned.

"You hear what a lot?"

"That I go a lot deeper than expected." He licked his lips. "Women are constantly surprised by me."

My face flushed at the innuendo. He grinned, waiting for me to react. I didn't want to give him the satisfaction, but as that self-congratulatory expression crossed his face, I realized that I wasn't going to be able to resist.

"I'm guessing the women you've been impressing haven't used the Magnum 2000." I smiled sweetly. "That dildo has gone deeper than any cock I know could." I looked down at the front of his pants. "And judging by the bulge—or lack thereof—that I saw in the front of your swimming shorts this morning, I'd say that yours isn't even up for comparison." My heart was racing as I finished up my little speech.

Annoyance flashed across his face, but he covered it quickly with amusement. "You have absolutely no idea, old maid. We better go inside and speak to Chuck before I give you grounds to sue me for sexual harassment, or even worse, get us locked up for a public display of wanton sexual activity."

"Excuse me?" I blinked at him. "What does that mean?"

"It means that if I were to let you feel or see just how big my magnum is, you'd be dropping to your knees for a nice long suck. And let's just say that my lollipop lasts for a very long time." He winked.

Before I could respond he was opening the door and walking into the building, with me straggling behind him. And the only thought on my mind was, just how big was he? And would he taste as good as I thought he looked?

CHAPTER 8

I was woken up by sunlight pouring through the window. I smiled as I stretched in the comfortable bed. I rolled over and yawned. I'd slept well.

Maybe the job wasn't going to be as bad as I thought. Wade and I had shared a pizza in the pub along with some drinks, and while he hadn't exactly opened up to me like we were best friends, we'd had a good time. At least, I thought we had. Not that it had gotten very personal. Wade had talked more about his business, and I'd asked him questions related to my duties. Even though it included a lot of tedious work, the job seemed like it could be rewarding. And once I had all the money, I could focus on living my life the way I really wanted to. I reached over to the nightstand and grabbed my notebook and pen and started scribbling a poem that was in my mind.

· · ·

Just one look
Just one touch
Just one feel
It wouldn't be too much
I can see it in your eyes
I can taste it on my lips
If you had your way
I'd be on my knees
I wouldn't say no
I wouldn't say yes
If it were just one night
I'd take off my dress

I paused as my heart raced and blushed at the thought of stripping naked for Wade. There had been one moment the night before that had made me feel as if the room were spinning. We'd both reached for a slice of pizza and our fingertips had grazed each other. It had barely been anything, but that touch and the subsequent look Wade had given me had felt like a jolt of lightning. My entire body had reacted, had been on alert, and as he'd talked, I'd been more drawn to his words and his body. Wade Hart was magnetic. With his handsome face, tall, built body, smooth voice, and devious smile, he had the ability to draw you to him, even if you didn't want to be drawn. When we'd arrived home, he'd gone straight to his room and I'd gone to mine, but as I'd gotten into bed, I'd lain there and wondered what I would do if he knocked and walked in naked.

A sudden knocking on the door interrupted my thoughts and I let out an involuntary yelp.

"Everything okay?" Wade walked into the room, in a pair of red swimming trunks and a bare chest. He wasn't naked, but my heart still raced as I sat up. He walked over to the bed and looked at me, notebook still in my hand. "Did something happen? Why did you yell?"

"Nothing happened, you just shocked me when you knocked on the door."

"Knocking on the door shocked you?" He raised an eyebrow. "Okay, then."

"Okay, so was there something you wanted?" I tried not to blush as I found myself once again staring at his chest. It was nicely tanned with a smattering of dark hair across his pecs. My fingers itched to run across it to see if the hair felt soft or prickly, but of course I didn't let them.

"I'm going for my morning swim." He smirked as if he knew what I was thinking. "I'll expect breakfast to be ready for me in 45 minutes."

"Okay." I looked over at the clock on the night table. "So, 8 a.m.?"

"Yes." He nodded. "Moving forward, I'll expect coffee to be ready for me before my swim."

"Uhm, okay? Do you have a coffee machine?"

"I have a machine, but I expect you to brew it and make it as I like it."

"I thought you liked it black?"

"I expect to have a black coffee and a boiled egg and fruit ready for me before my swim."

"Just now you just said you wanted coffee before your swim." I glared at him, not even caring when the sheet fell down and exposed the fact that I'd gone to bed in a too-tight tank top and no bra. His gaze fell to my chest, but I didn't care. "Now all of a sudden when I say you can set the timer on your coffee maker, you need more than coffee?"

"Firstly, you never said that I could set the timer on the coffee maker, and secondly, what you say or want doesn't matter: you work for me."

84

"I knew I was being too kind thinking you weren't a jack-ass," I grumbled. "So, what, I'm working for you from 6 a.m. to midnight? Why don't we just say I work for you 24/7. Why even give me my own room? Why don't I just sleep with you so I can be at your beck and call all night as well?"

"Are you asking if you can join me in my bed?" He gave me a pointed look. "Are you trying to come on to me, Ms. Carter?"

"What the hell? What are you talking about? No, I'm not trying to come onto you!"

"Well, your nipples are pointing to attention, and you're asking to sleep in my bed ..."

I looked down at my chest and gasped. I knew my tank top was a bit tight, but I didn't realize that my nipples were hard and visible through the flimsy fabric. I grabbed the sheet and pulled it back up to cover me. "I was being face-tious," I made a face at him. "Look it up if you don't know what it means."

"I'm not looking anything up. I want my coffee, now." He grinned. "Oh, and I also have your uniform ready and waiting for you."

"My uniform?"

"Don't tell me you forgot already that you have to wear a uniform."

"No, but I really don't understand why."

"It's not for you to understand. It's for you to do." He turned around and walked towards the door. "I'll put your uniform in the kitchen. I expect you to be wearing it when I come in for breakfast."

"Am I meant to wear it all day?"

"That's up to you."

"Really? That's up to me now?"

"It's only required at certain times of the day."

"What times of the day?"

J. S. COOPER

"You're a smart girl, let's see if you can figure it out."

"You really get on my nerves, you know that, right?"

"Is that any way to talk to your boss?" He turned his head, gave me a little wink and walked out of the room. My pillow hit the doorframe about five seconds later and I groaned into my hands. I stared at the poem in my notebook and was about to scratch it out when instead I wrote a new one.

J ust a crack
of a smile
is all
you need
to rise back up
out of his control.

I was not going to let Wade Hart irritate me. Or annoy me. Or make me slap him. I was not going to let Wade Hart make me fantasize about him. Or want him. Or flirt with him. I was going to act professional. I was going to pretend he was the president of the United States of America and I was an intern (and not Monica Lewinsky, either). I would treat him with respect, as if he were my father's boss or something. I would not let him ruffle my feathers or make me mad or turn me on or make me scream.

"You need to try harder than this, Savannah," I mumbled as I rolled out of the bed and stretched. I plodded towards the bathroom door and stopped by the window to stare at the rising sun for a few more seconds. It had been a nice morning while it had lasted, but now I was back to work. I was going to put on my game face and act like this was the

86

best job I'd ever had in my life and Wade Hart was the best boss I could ever hope to have.

"Oh, hell to the no!"

I picked up the maid's outfit that was sitting on the chair. "That asshole has to be joking." I held up the flimsy black skirt, white apron and black shirt. "Who the hell does he think he is?" I threw the outfit back onto the chair and stomped over to the fridge. "Hell will freeze over before I wear a maid's outfit," I muttered as I opened the fridge door and pulled out the carton of orange juice.

A part of me wondered if I should call John Boy back and tell him that I'd changed my mind. Maybe investing a grand into his business would get me back twenty grand. "Yeah right, and maybe you'll be the next Julia Roberts." I rolled my eyes as I grabbed a glass. "In your dreams." I drank the orange juice and considered my options. I could go out to the pool right now, throw the uniform into the water, and tell him I was leaving and quit. Or I could put on the uniform and keep my paycheck.

I grit my teeth. The uniform was degrading. And it looked pretty slutty, though I supposed if I wore tights underneath it, it wouldn't look as sexy as if I had bare legs. A small smile crossed my face as an idea hit me. I could wear sexy fishnet stockings underneath the skirt and high heels, and that would really show Wade that he couldn't intimidate me whatsoever. I didn't have stockings on me, but I could try and get them in town or order a pair online. I'd love to see his face if I sauntered into his room with a button undone and a pair of sexy fishnets. He'd soon realize that not only had he not intimidated me, but that I was comfortable in my own skin.

I put the glass down on the counter and walked back over to the table and grabbed the uniform. I walked slowly back to my room and stared at the paintings on the walls. Some of them looked real and expensive. I wondered if they were prints or if Wade had really spent millions on these works of art. It would be unreal to be so rich that I could afford to buy a Picasso or a Chagall. I couldn't even afford to buy the prints of great works of art at museum stores.

I opened the bedroom door and pulled off my top and jeans quickly before pulling on the uniform. The skirt was a lot shorter than I'd thought. I studied my reflection in the full-length mirror. I looked like a maid in a porno movie, not someone who actually cleaned for a living. But I wasn't a cleaner. And I wasn't a maid, either. I'd taken a job as an assistant. It was rude of Wade to expect me to wear this. I could feel myself growing angry again, so I quickly pulled out my phone to call Lucy so that she could calm me down and remind me why I was sticking at this job.

"Hey, sunshine, how's it going?"

"It's not going."

"Uh oh, what happened?"

"Did I tell you I hate my boss?"

"What did he do now?"

"He gave me my uniform."

"That bad?"

"Well, do you call a maid's uniform bad or not?"

"Oh, wow!" Lucy laughed and I glared into the phone.

"It's not funny."

"I know, I'm sorry, but man, this guy sounds like a piece of work."

"He's more than a piece of work, he's the biggest asshole I've ever met."

"Are you unhappy?" Lucy asked in a concerned tone. "You know you can always come home. We can figure it out if you're really hating it. We can move to another apartment, and maybe I can try and get a bartending job to help pay more."

"Lucy, you would get a second job to help me?"

"Of course. You're my best friend, Savannah. We can make this work. You can't stay at a job if you're uncomfortable."

"I wouldn't say I'm uncomfortable. I'd just say that my new boss sucks."

"So, should I expect you on the next train or not?"

"No." I sighed. "I can suck it up and be his maid even though I'm not actually his maid."

"Are you guys not getting on at all?"

"I thought we were last night. We had a good night, and I actually thought maybe this might not be so bad."

"Oh, tell me more."

"Girl, I would, but I have to go." I looked at the clock on my nightstand. "I have to hurry back to the kitchen and make his breakfast. If he gets out of the pool without food waiting for him on the table, he might just fire me, and then it won't matter if I'm annoyed with him."

"Oh, Savannah, you sound like this man's slave more than his personal assistant." Lucy sounded motherly as her voice got softer. "Look, if at any time you want to come home, just call, okay? Even if you don't have money. I will send you money for the train. I will send an Uber to the house. Shit, I'll rent a car and come and pick you up. You do *not* have to stay there, no matter what you think, okay?"

"Okay," I said almost tearfully. "Thank you, Lucy. I love you."

"I love you too, girl. Sisters for life."

"Best friends for life." I grinned into the phone and then

groaned. "Okay, I better go now for real. I have no idea what I'm going to cook. Maybe eggs and arsenic."

"If the police call me, I'll say I know nothing." She laughed as I hung up the phone and hurried back to the kitchen. I had fifteen minutes to get Wade's breakfast ready. I sighed as I opened the fridge and looked at its contents. I could see a carton of milk, eggs, bacon, sausages. I walked over to the bread bin and saw a loaf of sourdough bread. I could make scrambled eggs with bacon and toast. My stomach growled as I thought of those items.

"Scrambled eggs it is." I smiled to myself and walked back over to the fridge and took out four eggs and some milk. I opened the cupboard to find a pan and bowl and I found myself humming under my breath as I worked. It wasn't actually so bad making breakfast in the morning, especially when it was in a kitchen like this. The countertops were the white and gray Carrara marble that I loved and a giant slab of the same material adorned the massive island. I turned on the eight-burner Miele stovetop and admired my surroundings. French doors led out to the back garden, and it looked like it was going to be a sunny day. I felt content. Which surprised me considering I was in the middle of nowhere cooking breakfast for a man who annoyed the shit out of me.

I placed a frying pan on top of one of the burners and melted some butter in the pan as I cracked open the eggs and added a dash of salt, pepper, and milk to the eggs before whisking them together. As I beat the eggs, I looked around for a microwave. I was debating frying the bacon or heating it up in the microwave in some paper towels.

"To fry or not to fry that is the question." I giggled to myself as I poured the eggs into the pan and quickly looked for a spatula.

"Sorry, what was that?" Wade's deep voice sounded from behind me.

I turned around to see him standing at the edge of the kitchen, his hair dripping wet and a large white towel wrapped around his waist.

"I was talking to myself." I turned back to the eggs and scrambled them in the pan. I could hear him walking towards me and I looked up to his face with a pleasant smile on my face. "Breakfast will be ready in about five minutes. Would you like one or two slices of toast, sir?"

"Two." He grinned, his eyes close to mine as he stopped next to me. I could see how light the inner irises were compared to the outer circle. I'd never seen so many brilliant shades of green in one pair of eyes. "I see you found your uniform."

"Yes, I did." I pressed my lips together before I said something else.

"So, you like it?"

"Do I like being dressed up as a maid?" I cocked my head to the side. "What do you think?"

"I don't know. That's why I'm asking."

"Is this some sort of bad joke?" I rolled my eyes.

"Am I laughing?"

"Who knows? Maybe you're laughing inside at how ridiculous I look."

"I think you look quite stylish and pretty." His eyes surveyed my legs. "If you want to wear this all day, I have no problems with it."

"Why don't I wear it into town as well, while I do the shopping?"

"If you want." He laughed and I just shook my head. "I'm hungry. When will the food be ready?"

"I already told you it will be done in about five minutes. Why don't you go and change into some dry clothes and stop dripping water on the kitchen floor? By the time you're done, breakfast will be ready."

"Sounds like a good plan." He smiled and lightly touched me on the shoulder. "And to answer your question, you should fry the bacon, always fry the bacon." He winked and then walked out of the kitchen.

I couldn't stop myself from staring at his strong back as he walked out, then I took a deep breath as I walked to the fridge to get the bacon. Wade Hart was a lot of things, annoying, cocky, and self-centered, but more than anything, he was sexy as hell.

☙❧

"Thank you for breakfast. That was delicious." Wade finished his last piece of toast and smiled. "If you want to create a menu for the week today and present it to me, I can go over it and make any changes I see fit."

"Sure, I can do that." I continued eating my toast and reached for my cup of coffee. "So, am I going to be spending most of my time as your housekeeper, then?" I sipped on my coffee and studied his face. "That's fine. You can pay me for whatever you want, but I just want to be clear about my duties as I feel like I may have had a different understanding of what this job was going to be."

"I thought I made it quite clear that you would be splitting chores between the office as my assistant and the kitchen as my cook."

"Just checking you weren't also going to be adding bedroom duties like your whore as well, or something."

"Like my whore?" He tilted his head to the side and laughed. "What would give you that idea?"

"Nothing gave me that idea, I just wanted to check is all."

"I don't need to pay for sex. I don't need whores. So no, I won't be needing you in my bedroom performing any duties." He stood up and laughed. I looked up at him and swallowed hard. He was right, of course, a man as hot as him could have any woman he wanted, even if he was poor. Given that he was also rich as hell, I was sure he had no issues. "But if you want to pay me a visit at night so that I can fulfill any needs you may have, be sure to let me know." He winked. "It seems like you might need training in many different ways."

"What the hell is that supposed to mean?" Did he know I was a virgin? Was I that obvious? My face grew red as I stared at him as he towered over me.

"Just saying if you want a more intimate piece of The Wade Hart, you only need to ask."

"Let's just say that anyone that has *The* in front of their name is not someone I want to be intimate with." I stood up, and while I still had to crook my neck to look up at him, I didn't feel like he was overpowering me like I had while I'd been sitting down. "So don't bother trying to come to my room for any fun. I'm not interested."

"Really?" He took a step closer. "You're telling me you could resist a piece of this." He held his t-shirt out and then bent down so that his lips were close to mine. A part of me thought he was going to kiss me, right here, right now and all I could think about was if I had any bacon caught between my front teeth. "Savannah …"

I could feel his breath against my lips as he said my name and if my heart had beat any faster, it could have given Usain Bolt a run for his money.

"Yes, Wade?"

This was the moment, he was going to kiss me, I could

feel it. I would allow him to kiss me for five, ten seconds max, and then I would push him away.

"You can work in the library today, while we wait on your desk," he said, a teasing expression in his eyes. "Do the dishes, and then you can change if you want, and you can start on the menus. I'll come into the office later, and we can discuss some of your other duties. I want you to make a database of all the US, UK, and Canadian charities that are doing work in Kenya, Uganda, and Tanzania, and I'll tell you what info I will need for each charity."

"Okay." I blinked as he pulled away from me, disappointed that he hadn't kissed me. I tried to ignore the fact that the air between us smelled like him, a manly scent of body wash and cologne that made me want to pull him over to me so that I could bury my face in his chest. What was wrong with me? Why was I acting and feeling so desperate to touch this man?

"Good." He nodded and smiled. "Also, I was just joking earlier. Obviously, you wouldn't want anything with me. You have your boyfriend to think about, don't you?"

"Oh, yeah." My face went beet red. I'd already forgotten I'd told him I had a boyfriend. This was why it was bad to lie. It was inevitable that a liar would forget their lies at some point. I just hadn't realized that it would be so quickly for me. I cleaned up the kitchen quickly and then hurried to my room, where I changed into a pair of faded jeans and my Columbia sweater. I wasn't exactly wearing office attire, but I didn't care. If I had to wear a maid's uniform part of the day, I was going to wear whatever I wanted during the other part.

The library was exactly what I'd expected to find in a huge house like this. It was grand and contained hundreds of books. There was a large oak table in the center of the room that looked out to a bay window that showcased what appeared to be multiple rose bushes of different colors. I took a seat at the table, opened the laptop, and sat back. As I waited for the screen to load, I stood up and walked over to one of the bookshelves and ran my fingers across a stack of red leather-bound books on birds. I pulled one out and opened it up to a random page and read out loud, "The eastern bluebird is a small migratory thrush found in open woodlands, farmlands, and orchards ..."

The text was accompanied by a beautiful watercolor picture of the bluebird. I flicked through the book to look at more photos of birds before closing it and walking to the other side of the room and gazing at a different set of books. I found two black-bound volumes that looked out of place and pulled one off of the shelf. It was slightly padded and I opened it to see a stack of photos and handwritten letters. I looked towards the door wondering if Wade would be upset if he knew I was going through the books but quickly pulled the stack out anyway. The top photo showed a handsome man who looked almost identical to Wade, all tall and dark and strong. He was standing next to a beautiful petite blonde with a beguiling smile and flowery pink dress. He had his arm around her waist, and he was staring down at her lovingly while she looked directly into the camera. Was she Wade's mom? Whoever she was, she was beautiful. I picked up one of the letters and opened it up. A pressed rose that fell out and I bent down to pick it up. I scanned the letter, wondering if I was overstepping my bounds.

.   .   .

"*To my darling Louisa,*

Has it really been four weeks since I have seen you? I feel like my heart will not go on if I don't get to see you soon. Papa has told me that he wants us to go sailing in Europe next summer, and all I can think is that I couldn't bear to live another summer without you. Say you will marry me, my love. I know you wanted me to propose in a romantic fashion and I still will, but I cannot hold back. I feel as if I were a man off at war with his true love back home. I think about you always. Be true to me, my dear.

Yours always and forever,
Joseph Hart

I grabbed for the next letter, feeling emotional as I finished reading the first one and eager to read more of their love story. I was about to open it when Wade walked into the library. I jumped back in surprise.

"Hey." Wade's eyes narrowed as he stared at me with the black book in my hand, but he didn't say anything about it. "I thought we could go into town, grab lunch, and then I could go over some of the charity database information I needed you to gather."

"Go into town for lunch? We just ate."

"I need to pick up a package that's at the post office, and I figured you could do some grocery shopping."

"But we haven't discussed the menus for the week yet."

"Why don't you surprise me?"

"I didn't think you were the sort of guy who liked to be surprised." Which was an understatement. Wade seemed like the most Type A person I'd ever met in my life. I bet he was a Taurus as well, bullheaded as could be, or maybe he was a Scorpio. Scorpios always seemed to think they knew everything. Not that I was going to ask him, though. I didn't want him to think I was crazy. What sort of person lived their life by star signs? Not that I lived my life by them, of course, but I did think that people of the same sign were generally alike.

"Wow, I didn't know I was that transparent. You've barely known me 48 hours and yet you seem to know all about me."

"I wouldn't even pretend to guess I knew even one-tenth of the man you are, Wade." I shook my head and realized that his eyes were now on the book in my hand. "I was just looking." I couldn't keep a note of defensiveness out of my voice.

"Okay.' He shrugged. "You can look at whatever books you want to."

"I found a letter and some photos in this one." I held the letter up. "I think they were your parents'. Do you want them?"

"Do I want what?" He frowned. "My parents?"

"No, their letters and the photographs."

"No." His voice was stilted. "My dad is dead, and my mom, well, she's in France."

"I'm sorry." My heart softened for him. "Your mom must have been devastated when he died."

He laughed, but it was a dark sound that expressed more anger than happiness. "She's the one who killed him." He took in my shocked expression. "Not physically, of course. My mother can barely lift her hand for a manicure, let alone a gun or a knife to kill anyone."

"Oh, okay." I wanted to ask him what he'd meant, but he'd already started walking to the door.

"Check your email. I sent you some files you need to print out. Open the cupboard to the right and you'll see a printer. The laptop is already connected to the network. I'll meet you downstairs in thirty minutes."

"Okay." I walked back to the table. I took a seat, but Wade didn't leave. "Did you need anything else?"

"No." He shook his head as he stood in the doorway and studied me. His eyes took in my attire and I wondered if he was going to ask where the maid's uniform was, but he didn't. "I'll see you downstairs."

And with that he was gone, leaving me to wonder what his comment about his mom had meant. His parents had been so in love. At least his dad had. His dad was the one gazing at the mom lovingly, and it was the dad that had written the letter. Had it been a one-sided love affair then? Was that what Wade had meant? I wanted to read the rest of the letters, but I had to get some work done first. I needed to print out the attachments he'd sent me, and I also needed to google some recipes because I had absolutely no idea what I was going to be cooking for the rest of the week.

❧

The sweet Southern drawl of a country singer spilled through the speakers in the cute little cafe we sat in. I had the menu in my hands, and Wade was texting someone on his phone. The tablecloth was a bright pink and orange paisley design. A small jar of sunflowers sat in a unique glass vase in the center of the table. Big prints of old movie posters hung on the wall, and in one corner sat a jukebox that looked like it had come right out of the '60s.

"Welcome to Herne Hill Cafe, where the food is good and the coffee's better. How can I help you today?" An older lady wearing a pale pink uniform that clashed with her purple hair walked up to the table. "Why, Wade Hart, is that you?"

"Hello, Beryl, how are you doing today?" Wade put his phone on the table and smiled at the lady. "This is my new assistant, Savannah. I'm sure you'll be seeing a lot of her around here."

"Hey there, Savannah, you from Georgia?" She asked with an eager smile. "I'm from Duluth."

"No, I live in the city, but I'm originally from Florida."

"You'll like working for Mr. Hart." She beamed at me and then batted her eyelashes at Wade. "I saw Henry in here two weeks ago. He said he's visiting."

"He is." Wade nodded.

"He's not staying at the manor?"

"You know he never stays at the manor." Wade laughed and Beryl raised an eyebrow. I stared at them for two seconds trying to figure out why Beryl's face looked so taken aback. "Now will you give us a few moments to discuss your menu?"

"Yes, Mr. Hart." Beryl blushed, glanced at me, and stepped back. I watched as she hurried to the kitchen and my eyes moved to Wade.

"Why doesn't Henry stay with you when he visits?"

"He can't comment on what he doesn't see and vice versa."

"What?" I blinked. "Are you talking in code or trying to rhyme?"

"Did I rhyme?" He grinned. "And if I did, is that a crime?"

I groaned at his comment. "I'm just trying to understand why Henry doesn't stay with you. You have a huge house."

"I have a huge house, but I like things a certain way. And so does Henry. It's healthier for our relationship to live apart."

"What about family holidays?"

"What are those?" He raised an eyebrow. "We didn't all grow up in a nuclear family that followed traditional customs, you know, Savannah."

"You didn't celebrate Christmas or Thanksgiving or Easter?"

"My family wasn't big on holidays." He shook his head. "Have you decided what you want to eat?"

I wasn't going to let him change the subject. "Did you and Henry not grow up together, then?" I'd been under the impression that they were close, but maybe I'd been incorrect.

"We grew up together."

"Are you close?"

"You're nosey."

"I prefer curious."

"You know that curiosity—"

"Killed the cat." I interrupted him. "Yes, I know, and I'm lucky I'm not a cat."

"Funny." He pointed to my menu. "What do you want to eat?"

"What's the deal with you and Henry?"

"Henry is my best friend." He shrugged. "There's no story. We both just like to keep our nocturnal and other activities private, that's all."

"Nocturnal activities?" I frowned.

"Do I really need to spell it out?" He licked his lips and winked. "I think you know what I mean."

"Oh." I blushed. "So, do you have a girlfriend then? Does Henry?"

"You're awfully interested in Henry's life for someone that insists she doesn't care about him."

"I don't care about him. I'm just curious."

"We're both single." He grinned. "And I don't see that changing anytime soon. We both like our freedom too much."

"You think being in a relationship would take away your freedom?"

"I don't think. I know." He waved Beryl back over to the table. "I hope you're ready to order because I'm hungry."

"Liar," I muttered under my breath.

He chuckled, his green eyes lighting up as he threw his head back. I looked back down at my menu and put the rest of my questions to the back of my mind.

"You guys ready?" Beryl pulled out her notepad from the front of her apron and a pen from behind her ear. "What do you want?"

Wade nodded towards me. I glanced at the menu again quickly. "I'll have the lasagna, please."

"Maybe not, dear." Beryl shook her head and I stared at her in confusion.

"Do you not have it today?"

"Oh, we have it."

"So, then I'd like to order the lasagna, please?"

"Is she slow?" Beryl looked over at Wade and then made a face. "Or is that one of those words we're not meant to use anymore?"

"What?" I said. I could see that Wade was trying not to laugh. "I'm not sure what's going on."

"My dear," Beryl sounded out each word slowly. "I don't know if you're some sort of dummy, but what would you like to eat?"

"I said lasagna." I bit down on my lower lip to stop myself from adding *bitch!* And to think that I'd thought she'd been such a sweet older lady just seconds ago.

"And I said I think not."

"Okay." I shook my head. Obviously, this was going nowhere. "I'll have the chicken fried steak, then."

"Hmmm." She made a face. "I don't think so."

"The meatloaf?"

"Girl."

I looked over to Wade who was now laughing silently. I glared at him. He just smiled back at me and I sighed loudly.

"What do you recommend, then?"

"Well, we have a variety of world-class dishes." She beamed at me happily. "You can't really go wrong with any of them."

"Really? So then, I'll have the las—"

"We'll have two burgers," Wade cut me off. "I'll have bacon and cheese on mine." He looked over at me. "You want bacon and cheese?"

"Just cheese." I pursed my lips. "And I'll have the burger medium."

"We'll take the burgers medium-well." Wade cut me off again. "And we'll take an order of fries and onion rings."

"Sounds good." Beryl nodded. "I'll have that out to you in a few minutes."

"I'll have a cup of coffee as well, please," I added quickly.

"We'll take two of your finest Cokes," Wade said with a smile.

I shook my head as Beryl walked away. "Okay, what the hell is going on here?" I asked, my tone a little sharp. "I didn't want a burger."

"Honey, Beryl and I were doing you a favor. Her husband Peter is the chef, well, I guess I'd say cook, and there's only one dish he can make that tastes good." He grinned. "The man knows how to drop some frozen fries and onion rings, and he knows how to cook up a burger on the stovetop. His other dishes, not so good."

"What the ... Are you joking?"

"Do I look like I'm joking?"

"So basically, the only items you can get at this cafe are burgers and fries?"

"They make a damn good burger and fries." He grinned.

"And anyway, you're the chef at home, so we don't need to worry about eating here too much."

"Yeah." I bit down on my lower lip. I should just keep my mouth shut because my skills in the kitchen weren't all that either. "Oh yeah, you never told me some of your favorite dishes so I could try and make them for dinner some evenings." I paused and looked at him. "What meals did you say you were preparing for yourself again?"

"What are you talking about?" He stared at me blankly.

"When we first talked about the job, you said you were going to make your own breakfasts or dinners or something?" I smiled at him weakly, wishing I could remember exactly what he'd said.

"Hmm," He shook his head. "I don't remember that. You're responsible for all meals. That's why I'm paying you so much, remember?"

"That's not how I remember it." I could hear my voice growing colder. "When am I supposed to have any time to myself?"

"To do what? Call your boyfriend on the phone?"

"I do need to talk to and see other people."

"You can invite him to come up if you want to." He shrugged. "I'd like to meet the man that can put up with your smart mouth."

"Put up with my smart mouth? I'll have you know that he likes my mouth just fine, thank you very much."

"I'm sure he does." He leaned forward. "It looks like you can open it quite wide, though I don't know if that's an issue with him."

"What are you talking about?"

"I don't want to be crude, but I think you know what I mean." His eyes bore into mine. "Maybe your boyfriend isn't working with much, so it never mattered how much you could fit in."

"Fit in?" I repeated his words. "Fit what in?" I stared back at him and then his meaning dawned on me. "Oh hell no." I blushed a deep red. "You're so damn inappropriate!" I sat back and pointed at him. "If I sue you, you're going to have to pay me a lot more than a hundred grand."

"Are you planning on suing me?" He raised an eyebrow. "Is that what you're saying?"

"No, of course not." I sighed. "You just need to remember that you just met me, and I'm your assistant, not some girl you met in a bar that you can just talk to however you want."

"You think that's how I talk to girls in bars?"

"It would explain why you're single." I smirked. "No matter how good looking you are, no girl is interested in a guy approaching her and talking about BJ's."

"BJ's?"

"Blowjobs," I said, almost too loudly, and blushed. "Don't even try and deny it. We both know that's what you were referring to when you were talking about my mouth."

"We do, do we?" He sipped on his water. "I would ask if you liked giving them, but I don't want to be any more inappropriate with you."

"Yeah, right." It was my turn to grab some water now. "I don't think you care about propriety whatsoever."

"You think you know me so well, don't you?"

"Actually, not at all." I shook my head as I stared at him. "What do you do for fun? Do you live here full time?"

"So many questions." He chuckled, but I could tell he didn't like to talk about himself.

"Well, not really. I asked you two questions. That's not exactly a litany."

"Using your Ivy League words on me, huh?" Wade teased.

I realized that this was his way of changing the subject.

Why did he dislike talking about himself so much? Most men I knew—in fact, most people generally— were always more than happy to talk about themselves.

"So, what do you do for fun?" I asked him again. "I told you about my poetry."

"Oh yes, my little Emily Dickinson."

"I'm nowhere near as good as Dickinson."

"I bet you are."

"I'm not."

"Let me hear one of your poems."

"Wade, I asked what you liked to do for fun. Stop trying to deflect and change the subject."

He stared at me as if he were thinking and then finally he answered me.

"I like hunting."

"Figures."

"What does that mean?"

"I'm not trying to judge you, but I don't like hunting because I don't believe in killing innocent animals. I've seen those videos of hunters going to Africa and killing nearly extinct rhinos and elephants. It's disgusting."

"I'm not a trophy hunter." He pursed his lips. "I would never go and shoot animals that are nearly extinct."

"But you do shoot for fun? Hunting is a sport for you?"

"I grew up hunting with my dad."

"And that makes it okay?"

"I feel like you don't even want to hear what I have to say." He sighed. "All I said is I like hunting. Maybe I hunt rodents or cockroaches."

"Who hunts cockroaches?" I rolled my eyes.

"Maybe I do." He grinned, and I just shook my head.

"Well, you hunt them and then eat them." I smiled at him sweetly. "That's something I'd love to see."

"I can do that if you cook them for me."

"Eww, no! I don't even want to see a cockroach, let alone cook them." I pretended to throw up. "That's so gross."

"Are you discriminating against cockroaches?"

"Are you an idiot?"

"Is that any way to talk to your boss?" He tapped his finger on the table.

"No, sir, sorry, sir, won't happen again, sir."

"Good, good." His eyes crinkled and we both ended up with a smile on our faces. "You have a good sense of humor. I like that."

"Thank you." Despite myself, I was flattered by the compliment.

"It's a pity you have a boyfriend." His stare grew more intense and my scalp prickled a little.

"Why is that?" I swallowed as I waited for his response.

"Well, because I wouldn't be able to do this ..." He said as he stood up and walked over to me.

"Do what?"

Time seemed to slow as he leaned down and pressed his lips against mine. He kissed me for a few seconds, his lips warm and firm. My eyes widened and my skin flushed, but before I had a chance to react, he straightened back up.

"That." He grinned at me. "I'll be right back."

And with that, he walked to the back of the café. I sat there rubbing my lips and wondering what the hell had just happened.

"Hey, I actually have to stay in town longer than I thought today." Wade walked back to the table a moment later. "I can get you a car back home or you can roam around the town. I'll give you the rest of the day off."

"Sounds good to me." I was hoping he would explain to me what he'd been thinking by kissing me. Not that it had been a full-on makeout session or anything, but a kiss was still a kiss. I wanted to know if it had meant anything to him.

"Feel free to explore the town and I'll give you the number to a car service to get home. Here's a set of keys if you get home late."

"Oh, thanks. I guess I don't want to wake you up."

"Oh, you won't wake me up. I might not be home when you get back."

"Oh?" I waited for him to tell me more, but Beryl chose that moment to return with our burgers.

"Here we are, folks, two of our finest grilled cheeses. Hope you enjoy them!" She gave us a cheerful smile.

"Grilled cheese? But—" I started but Wade shook his head as he sat down.

"Thanks, Beryl, looks great." He grabbed a fry from his plate and munched down on it as an admittedly delicious-looking grilled cheese was placed in front of me.

"Thanks." Once again I felt like I was in the Twilight Zone. "Okay, what's going on here?" I looked at Wade and raised an eyebrow. "Did we or did we not order burgers? And actually, I ordered lasagna, but you told me just take the burger because that is what they are known for."

"Savannah, you have to understand that you're in Herne Hill Village now, not the big city. Things work differently here."

"What the hell does being in a small village have to do with it? Shouldn't I be able to order what's on the menu and actually get it?" I grabbed the grilled cheese and took a bite. The warm American cheese oozed into my mouth along with the perfectly crisp sourdough bread. "This is delicious," I said as I took another bite and grabbed a French fry.

"See, it is as it was meant to be." He grinned and took another bite. "Sometimes life doesn't go according to plan, but it always goes the way that it should."

"I guess so ..." I grabbed another fry. "So, you won't be home tonight?"

"Tonight, tomorrow morning … Who's to say?" He winked at me and then sat back. "I'm a busy man."

"Have a date?" I asked him lightly, trying to pretend I wasn't interested in the answer, but I could tell from his cocky grin in response that he knew my question wasn't that innocent.

"Wouldn't you like to know?" he sniffed.

With that, I decided to ignore him for the rest of the meal. If he could play hot and cold, so could I. Let Wade Hart try and kiss me again, I'd slap him across the face and tell him to have a good day.

"What I'd really like to know about are your parents," I said. "The love letter your dad wrote to your mom, it was so sweet. So loving. It must have been amazing growing up with parents so in love."

"*So in love?*" He mimicked my words, his face twisting cruelly. "Do you want to know the truth of my parents' relationship, Savannah?"

"Yes." I nodded, surprised at the vehemence in his voice.

"My dad loved my mother, he loved her so much that when she left him to flee to Paris to make it as a model and hook up with designers and nobility, she broke his heart. She broke his heart into a million pieces. My mother was a socialite. At the end of the day, all she cared about was her looks and being adored by as many men as possible. She never loved my father. She only loved herself. And when he realized that, he died. He died because he didn't want to keep living. He died of a broken heart. He wasted away into nothing, and I will never forgive her for that."

Wade's voice sounded hollow, and I felt like I was glimpsing a softer side to him, a deeper side that made me look at him as someone other than my cocky, sexy, and completely arrogant boss. I saw him as a man with issues. A man with a past. A man with more depth and more pain than I ever would have imagined. After reading the letter this morning and seeing the photograph, it had struck me that his father must have truly been very heartbroken. He'd loved Wade's mom so very much. And it hadn't been enough.

If a man ever loved me that much, I'd find it very hard to walk away.

CHAPTER 9

"There are a lot more people here than I thought there would be," I whispered into the phone. I took a nervous sip of red wine.

"Makes sense, it's a small town. I bet all the locals go there." Lucy sounded cheerful. I could hear the sounds of the television in the background. "Did you decide what poem you were going to recite tonight?"

"No." I sighed. "I'm shocked I signed up, to be honest. You know how I feel about performing in new places."

"It will be great. Hey, hold on a second. Jolene, no! Jolene put it down, Jolene!" she yelled. I made a face wondering what my dog was up to now. "Hey, sorry about that."

"What happened?"

"Jolene grabbed a slice of my pizza and ran." She made a tut-tutting sound. "That dog is really too much."

"I'm sorry, Lucy."

"It's not your fault," she replied, but I knew she did think it was my fault. She didn't think I had trained Jolene well as a puppy, but I had tried my best. "So, how's it going with bossman?"

"Bossman still sucks." I lowered my voice. "But something interesting happened today."

"What?"

"He kissed me."

"He *what*?" Lucy screeched. "How did you not start the conversation with this information?"

"Well, I didn't want to make it seem like a big deal." I took another sip of wine. "I mean it wasn't like a full-on pash."

"What?" Lucy sounded confused.

"Full-on pash."

"What the hell is a pash, Savannah?"

"Remember that Australian show we watched where they called making out pashing?"

"No, I don't, and stop changing the subject. Your boss kissed you, and what did you do back?"

"I kissed him back." I paused and then giggled slightly. "Okay, I mean, maybe I'm exaggerating a bit. His lips pressed against mine for five seconds and I didn't push him off."

"That's it?" Lucy sounded exasperated. "Girl, that's not a kiss."

"Well, it was *something*," I shot back, embarrassed that I was probably making something out of nothing.

"Talk to me when he's going down on you under the kitchen table or you're giving him a BJ in a restaurant." Lucy giggled. "That's the sort of session I want to be hearing about."

"He's not going to go down on me in the kitchen."

"Girl, then is he even worth it?"

"I never said he was."

"You know what our problem is, Savannah?" Lucy sounded all matter-of-fact, and I sat up.

"No, what?"

"We're too inexperienced and immature. How do we expect to find real men and have real, passionate relationships if we're still acting like kids?"

"Who's acting like a kid?"

"Girl, your boss barely pecked you and you were acting like you guys filmed some sort of X-rated video."

"I never acted like we made an X-rated video!" I huffed.

"You either want in his pants or not, and if you do, then you need to go for it." She giggled and my eyes narrowed. Was she drunk?

"Are you drinking, Lucy?"

"No." She hiccupped.

"Really?"

"Well, maybe I made myself a martini." She laughed. "It doesn't taste like a martini, but it sure is strong."

"Oh, Lucy!" I laughed out loud. "I wish I was there getting drunk with you."

"I wish I was there with you about to go on stage and perform."

"You should go to an open mic night in the Village. Maybe you'll meet someone."

"I don't want to meet anyone. At least not while I'm alone." She sighed. "I wish you were here."

"Awww, I'll be home soon, and then we can go on all sorts of adventures around the city because I'll have money then."

"Promise?"

"Promise!" I smiled into the phone. "I better go now, though. More and more people are starting to pour in and sit around the stage. I don't want to be that rude asshole still on their phone."

"Okay, call me later. Have fun and kill it, girl."

"Bye." I hung up and was surprised to find a younger-looking man standing in front of me with a grin on his face and a glass of Guinness in his hand.

"No one would think you're a rude asshole." He smiled. I blushed as he nodded at the seat next to me. "Is that seat open?"

"Yes." I gestured at it. "Please have a seat."

"New to town, right?" he asked as he sat down and drank from his stout.

"How did you know?" I asked in surprise.

"This is a small village. Everyone knows everything. You work up at Hart Manor?"

"Hart manor?" I raised an eyebrow. "I didn't know it was called that."

"That's what we locals call it." He chuckled. "You work for Wade?"

"Yes, do you know him?" I asked, wondering if the two men were friends. The guy next to me looked to be about my age. He wasn't terribly well-dressed, but he had a nice friendly smile and a warm personality.

"I know of him. Never met him." He shook his head and put his glass down. "I'm Gordon, nice to meet you." He held out his hand to me and shook it. "I want to say your name is Vanna or Vania?"

"Close, it's Savannah." I laughed. "The gossip train works fast."

"You're from Georgia?"

"Nope." I shook my head and wondered if Beryl had passed on that piece of incorrect information. "I'm from Florida, but I live in Manhattan right now—well, not *right* now. Right now, I live with Wade Hart. I'm his assistant."

"How do you like it?" He sounded curious.

"It's fine. He's fine." I shrugged and looked away. No way was I going to complain about my new boss to a stranger.

"Oh, you don't have to worry, I'm not going to say

anything. I'm fairly new to Herne Hill myself. Only been here about five years. I'm not a huge part of the rumor mill." He smiled congenially and lifted his glass. He had hazel eyes that seemed to sparkle and a mop of unruly jet-black hair. His boyish smile was infectious and I smiled back at him. "So, you're here for open mic night?"

"Yes, you?"

"Yup, I'm an actor and I like to act out monologues. The locals here hate it most of the time, but I have good fun. What are you going to do? Sing?"

"Sing? Ha! I can't sing to save my life. I will recite some of my poetry."

"Oh, awesome, I've never met a poet before." He took a long gulp of his drink, leaving a trace of white foam on his upper lip. He was a handsome man, too much of a boy for me, but I could see how many would find him attractive.

"I wouldn't say I'm a real poet. I just dabble, but I enjoy it."

"Don't be so modest. I bet you're great. What sort of poetry do you write?"

"Emotional and epic." I laughed. "And everything in between."

"Well, I'm super excited to hear it." He leaned back. "Welcome to town, by the way. It's always great to meet new people."

"Yeah, thanks." I sipped on my wine. "Can I ask you something?"

"Sure."

"Why did you move to Herne Hill Village if you want to be an actor?"

"Why? Do you think I won't catch my big break here?" He laughed. "I wanted to go to LA, but I had some unfinished business to take care of first."

"Oh, what sort of business?"

"Just family stuff." He shrugged. "My parents are from the village, and well you know how that can be ..." He took another sip of his drink. "Oh, look, Harry's about to go on the stage. The night is about to start."

I turned to face the stage and tried to quell the nerves in my stomach. There were a lot of people occupying the chairs now, ranging from what appeared to be young teens to seniors in their eighties and nineties. There was a buzz of excitement around the room, and I could see several people nervously shifting in their seats and whispering to their neighbors.

"Hey, everyone, welcome to Open Mic night. We have a full list tonight, so we're going to get started right away. Remember, if you need a new drink or some food, just come up to the bar and we'll serve you. To get the night started, we have Edith Shady performing the aria 'Nessun Dorma.' Edith, come on up."

I looked over to Gordon, who was grinning at me. "You're in for a treat."

"Oh, is she good?" I asked, wondering if everyone was going to be some sort of superstar asides from me.

"No, she's bloody awful." He winked. "If you have earplugs, I'd put them in now." He took two more deep gulps of his drink.

Edith, an elderly lady with purple hair and a white jumpsuit, began to screech an opera song that sounded vaguely familiar. I tried not to cringe. Instead, I drank from my wine glass and scrolled through my phone trying to decide which poems to recite. Suddenly, I noticed that the screeching had stopped and my name was being called. I stood up and headed to the stage, leaving my glass and phone on the table in front of me. I took the proffered microphone and smiled out into the crowd.

"Hi, everyone, my name is Savannah. I'm new in town.

I'm happy to be with you tonight and will read some of my original poetry." I looked into the faces in front of me and was pleased to see several nodding heads and smiling faces. Well, at least I knew they were listening to me. One friendly looking girl grinned at me, and Gordon gave me an encouraging nod. I took a deep breath and started to speak, my voice low with nerves in the beginning but growing louder as I gained my stride.

"I'm going to start with some of my shorter poems and end with a longer one.

"He didn't hear your tears,
        but
            that shouldn't be a surprise
    he never heard your
    laughter
    either."

A round of applause surrounded me. I paused and grinned, feeling like my poem had really been appreciated. I flung my right hand up and almost shouted into the mic as I started my second poem.

"RISE, my girl
        fly like the wind
            has caught your sail
    own your truth
    he might be gone, but
    your story
    still continues."

. . .

"You tell him, sister!" the girl who had grinned at me earlier shouted out. I laughed as I saw a few middle-aged men sitting at the bar, sipping on their beers and rolling their eyes. Middle-aged men weren't really my audience; in fact, men period weren't really my audience, but I didn't let that stop me.

"I like to call this one green," I said as inspiration hit me. "And I want you all to know that this is the first time I've ever performed this poem." In fact, it was the first time anyone would have ever heard it, including myself, because I was about to make it up on the spot.

"Green like emeralds,
    Hard as stone,
        They pierce me,
As if looking into my soul.
I thought I knew you,
You were so crass,
I thought you were just
Another self-centered ass.
But if I look beyond the leaves,
Behind the tall shaded bark
I can see that there's a scared boy
Who's trying to make his mark.
My heart doesn't know what to do,
My brain is fried
But the whispers in my head
Say to keep on trying.
Green like emeralds,
Envy sparkles too.
Hard as stone.
I really want to get to know you."

. . .

I paused and stared into the audience, my entire body on edge as Wade's face popped into my mind. He was consuming my thoughts, my dreams, my world. And now here I was, publicly reciting a poem about him. I stopped and smiled uncertainly into the crowd, waiting for them to respond.

"Bravo!" Gordon stood up and started clapping. I grinned at him and took a little bow as the rest of the crowd joined in. I made my way back to my seat and as I reached Gordon, I grabbed my wine glass and took a long deep gulp of my wine, finishing it off quickly.

"How do you feel?" he asked me as I sat down.

"Exhilarated, embarrassed, pumped." I leaned back. "But amazing." I smiled. "Really amazing."

"You did great." He looked surprised. I didn't know whether I should be offended or not.

"Did you not expect me to be good?"

"I expected your poems to be good." He smiled. "I just didn't expect that you would deliver them so passionately."

"I'm a different person when I recite poetry."

"I daresay that we all transform ourselves when we perform." He leaned towards me and his eyes searched mine for a few seconds. "Was that last poem about anyone in particular?"

"No, not really." I shook my head quickly.

"Aww, okay." He looked uncertain for a moment and an air of sadness seemed to pass over his face.

"You okay?" I asked, wondering what had upset him.

"Yes, I'm fine." He smiled congenially again. "I think that I will be called up next. You'll get to judge me for yourself."

"I bet you'll be great."

"Don't bet too much money." He laughed, and as he

threw his head back, it struck me how handsome he was. When I looked at him from a certain angle, he reminded me a bit of Wade. I shook my head and sighed. I was becoming obsessed with Wade, and that wasn't good. Obsession was close to mania, and I didn't want to become a maniac where Wade was concerned.

"We have another newcomer on stage tonight. Gordon, come on up," the MC announced, and Gordon jumped up. He walked up to the stage with a confidence that I envied, beaming into the crowd as he took the microphone.

"Hi, I'm Gordon. Tonight, I'm going to perform a piece from a play I wrote. I hope you enjoy it." He cleared his throat, placed the microphone back in the stand, and stood back. The lights dimmed, and a spotlight illuminated him on the stage. The crowd hushed, and I noticed that even the guys at the bar were staring at him in anticipation.

"What good am I if I don't have love?" Gordon's voice cracked, and he seemed to shrink into himself. "I go from here to there, and yet I feel as if I were nowhere." He was talking earnestly now. "My mother, my mother she believed in me. She loved me. She saw herself in me. She wanted me to achieve my dreams, but when I didn't, she crumbled. She crumbled more than me." He clenched and unclenched his fists, pacing back and forth on the stage. "And now, now I ask you to love me back, to have that same faith, same trust, and to you, I'm invisible." His breath caught and he coughed. He turned to look directly in front of him. "And yet, here I am talking to you as if you were here, as if you understood, as if you cared. What use is my life without love? I used to hate you, used to hate myself, why was I born into this body, why was I never good enough? Why? Just one change in our destinies. And it all could have been different. I could have been you and you could have been me. And then it would have been you begging me to love you. It would have been you wanting to be brave enough. It would have been you." A lone tear rolled down his face.

I held my breath, blown away by Gordon's talent. He was brilliant. I sat there in the audience, watching a man about to break down. And my heart ached for him. How awe-inspiring to have a talent to connect with people like that. A wry smile crossed his face as his eyes met mine for a few seconds. "I always wondered if I was someone that was incapable of being loved. Maybe I wasn't good enough. Maybe I was born cursed. Maybe the demons that torment my mind will never leave. But then I remember that I have known love. I have felt its bliss adorning my face. I have kissed the sweet lips of a gentle soul. And though I still wonder, ultimately, I know it will be worth it. I may never have your love, but you, you shall always have mine." He stopped then and burst into a huge grin as he walked back to the microphone. "Thank you, thank you."

We all burst into applause, my hands clapping along with everyone else's. The lights came back on, and a satisfied looking Gordon walked back to his seat next to me.

"You're amazing!" I said as he sat down. "You're one of the best actors I've ever met in my life."

"And how many actors have you met?"

"Not loads, but enough." I smiled. "You're really talented."

"Thank you, Savannah." He smiled, yet once again I could see that spark of sadness in his face. "I appreciate your kind words."

"You're welcome." I leaned over and squeezed his hand. He looked into my eyes and an unspoken emotion passed between us. Gordon was a kindred spirit; somehow, I knew he was meant to have come into my life. "I should get going soon, though. I don't want Wade to think I'm staying out all night, and I have to be up early to make his breakfast."

"To make his breakfast, huh?" Gordon chuckled and sat back. "Well, I guess he's a man who knows what he wants and has the money to pay for it."

"Yes, he does." I rolled my eyes and stood up. "It was nice meeting you, Gordon."

"And you too." He grabbed a napkin and a pen from his pocket and scribbled down some numbers. "Here are my digits. Feel free to text or call me at any time." He handed it to me and his phone and I input my number into his contacts. "We can grab a drink or dinner, or chat, or whatever." He stood up and reached over to hug me. "It was nice meeting you, Savannah Carter." He gave me a quick kiss on the cheek that made me blush, and I smiled my thanks at him. I put the napkin in my handbag and headed out of the bar. As I got outside and reached for my phone to call a car, Beryl headed over to me, a concerned look on her face.

"Well, hello, dear, having a good night?"

"Yes, thank you." I smiled at her, surprised that she was out at the pub.

"You off home then?" she mumbled. I nodded yes. "Good, good." She paused and then stepped a little closer to me. "You be careful with those Hart boys, you hear." Her eyes seemed to pierce into mine. "All that glitters is not gold."

"Uhm, okay." I nodded again.

"It's like lasagna, dear, you might want it very badly, but sometimes what you need is a burger."

"Uhm, okay." I didn't bring up the fact that she had actually given me a grilled cheese.

"They're nice boys, but secrets abound ..." She paused and looked around. "And when secrets abound, you know what happens." I was about to ask her what she meant when she suddenly gasped. "I should go. I'm singing tonight. See you around, sweetie."

"Bye." I gave her a quick wave and waited for the cab. Her words repeated in my mind. *Be careful with the Hart boys*, she'd said. Was she inferring that both Wade and Henry were bad eggs? And why would I have to be careful? I wished now that I'd asked her more questions, but given my experience at lunch with her, I wasn't sure that I would have received much of an answer.

CHAPTER 10

I paid the chatty cab driver and got out of the car before he could start asking me more questions about why I'd moved to Herne Hill Village. I walked to the front door quickly, took out my key, and opened the front door. I closed it quietly and then paused to see if I could hear any noises emanating from the house. The house was deadly quiet, and aside from the light on in the hallway, there didn't seem to be any other lights on in the house. I headed down the corridor towards the kitchen and wondered where Wade was. I opened the fridge and grabbed a bottle of water and then headed to the French doors to see if Wade was swimming. The pool was empty, so I headed back inside the house, slightly disappointed. I wiped my hair away from my forehead, feeling a bit sticky. It had been hot in the pub, and the weather here was humid. My hair was frizzy, and I knew that I needed a cool shower to feel better. As I headed back to my room I debated going for a swim but I didn't have that many hours to sleep if I was going to wake up early to cook Wade's breakfast.

I pulled up my top as I walked into my bedroom and

sank onto the bed. I wanted to call Lucy, but at this hour, she was most probably sleeping.

I lay there for a few seconds and sat back up. I needed to take a shower before I fell asleep. I yawned and jumped off of the bed. Where was Wade? Was he with someone? I bit down on my lower lip as I pictured him with another woman. What did I care? I stripped down to my bra and panties and headed to my en suite bathroom. The cool water in the shower felt amazing, and I massaged my scalp with the mango-scented shampoo that was already in the shower. I scrubbed my body quickly with the soap and rinsed myself off, grabbing a big white fluffy towel as I stepped out of the shower. As I headed back to the bedroom, I realized I wanted a cup of hot chocolate and decided to head to the kitchen to make it.

"Should I change first?" I stared down at my towel and then shrugged. Wade didn't seem to be home, so what did it matter? I walked back to the kitchen and turned on the kettle and started humming one of my favorite Adele songs as I waited for the water to boil. I opened the cupboard to look for the box of Swiss Miss hot chocolate packets I'd seen earlier when I heard a door open. My body froze as footsteps made their way towards the kitchen.

"Oh, shit." I looked over my shoulder as a bare-chested Wade came into view.

"Hey." He smiled as he headed towards me, wearing only a pair of red boxers. He looked at my wet hair and then down towards my bare feet and grinned. "Just had a shower?"

"Yup." I nodded. "I was just making some cocoa. I thought you were out."

"I'm not."

"I know that now." I clutched my towel closer to me. "When did you get in?"

"A while ago. You?"

"Maybe fifteen minutes ago." The kettle beeped indicating the water had boiled. "Do you want some tea or cocoa or anything?"

"I would love a cup of tea." He nodded as he took a step closer to me. "Do you normally head to the kitchen in just a towel?"

"I didn't think you were here."

"That doesn't answer my question."

"No, I don't normally walk around half-naked when I'm in the presence of strange men."

"I'm not a strange man, I'm your boss, and you're saying you're naked under that towel?"

"What do you think?" I raised an eyebrow and rolled my eyes, ignoring his quick laughter at my comment.

"Prove it to me."

"Prove what to you?"

"Prove to me that you're naked." There was a challenge in his green eyes as he stared at me. I looked back at him and ignored the smirk on his face as his lips twitched.

"You wish."

"Maybe I do." He took a step closer so that he was almost pressed against me. I could feel his body heat on my shoulders.

I swallowed. "Not going to happen." I shook my head.

"Are you blushing?" He touched my cheek lightly.

"No." I moved away from him to grab some cups. Why did he have this effect on me? Why did I just want to grab him and kiss him?

"How was the open mic night? Did you have fun?"

"I did have fun. I performed some poems."

"Oh, yeah?" His tone changed. "How did it go?"

"Pretty well, I think." I was going to tell him I made a friend but decided not to. "What type of tea do you want?"

"Anything decaffeinated, maybe a herbal tea?"

"Sure, let me look. Sugar or honey or anything?"

"No." He opened a cupboard next to me. "I'll get some cookies out as well."

"Oh, thanks." I looked toward him and smiled. "So, what did you do this evening?"

"You really want to know badly, don't you? You're quite nosey, Savannah Carter."

"I told you, I'm curious."

"If you must know, I was meeting up with a friend."

"I see." Was that code for he had a booty call with someone he considered a friend with benefits?

"How are you liking it here so far?"

"It's different but seems nice." I poured the water into the cups and looked over at him. "If I was more of a writer, I'd base a murder mystery here." I grinned. "It feels like the sort of village that Miss Marple would live in."

"Miss Marple? From the Agatha Christie books?"

"Yeah, have you read them?"

"No." He shook his head. "But I used to watch the British *Poirot* show with David Suchet. And know generally about her writing."

"Oh, I love her books." I grinned. "I'm an Agatha Christie addict. I have read all the books, listened to the audiobooks, and watched every movie made from the books."

"Wow, you really love her."

"I do." I handed him his cup and he took it from me with a small thank you. "Do you like reading?"

"I do." He nodded. "Do you want to sit down and chat for a little bit?"

"Oh, I don't know." I bit down on my lower lip. "I'm still in my towel."

"You can change." He smiled. "We can go into the living

room, relax on the couch, maybe you won't think of me as an ogre."

"I don't think of you as an ogre."

"You might if you could read my mind."

"Maybe I *can* read your mind," I teased him.

"Then what am I thinking?" He smiled and his eyes fell to the top of my towel.

"You're thinking you want to give me a raise." I laughed as my face grew red. *I know what you're thinking*, I thought. *You want to see me without my towel on*. And I knew that if he walked over to me and tugged on my towel, I would let it drop. And then I would wrap my arms around him, press my body into him and kiss him hard.

"Yeah, right." He laughed and shook his head. "Don't quit the day job to become a psychic."

"I'll try not to."

"Though I think I could be a psychic if I wanted to."

"Oh, yeah?"

"Yeah." He smirked. "I know what you're thinking."

"You do, do you?"

"Yup."

"What am I thinking?"

"You're thinking that if you weren't in a relationship, you'd be in my bed right now, with my head between your legs, and—" He started laughing as my face went beet red. "I'll stop there. I don't want to get you too hot and bothered."

"You're not getting me hot and bothered."

"Liar." He sipped on his tea. "You want me so badly right now that I bet the valley between your legs is wet, and not with water."

"Nope." I lifted my head high and ignored the sensitive feeling between my legs.

"Savannah, don't lie." He laughed. "If I were to touch

you right now, you couldn't resist me. You'd be like putty in my hands. You're lucky I'm a gentleman because I really want to touch you."

"Yeah, you're the one with the issue." I sipped on my hot chocolate. "I couldn't be less bothered by your presence or touch. I could spend the night in bed with you and not feel a thing."

"Oh, yeah?" He cocked his head to the side. "Is that true?"

"Yup." I tried to keep my voice light, though my hands were shaking slightly.

"Okay, then—show me."

"Show you what?"

"Spend the night in my bed, and let's see if you can keep your hands off of me."

"What are you talking about?" My heart was thudding. "I'm not sleeping with you."

"Why? Because you're scared you'll beg me to take you?"

"Ha, yeah, right. Not scared at all."

"Then let's do it." He took a step towards me. "If you're not bothered by me."

"I'm not."

"Sleep with me." He licked his lips. "Naked."

"No way." I shook my head vehemently. "Not going to happen."

"Fine, wear what you normally wear to bed. I'll keep my boxers on. If you're so sure you can resist me."

"Oh, I know I can resist you." I rolled my eyes. "That won't be a problem."

"Fine. Go and change." He reached for my cup. "I'll take your drink to my room."

"Fine. What do I get when I prove to you that I can resist you?"

"A five-grand bonus."

"Fine, that works for me." I feigned nonchalance. "This'll be the easiest five grand ever."

"That's what I thought." He stepped back. "Well, go and change and meet me in my room."

"Fine." I shrugged. "See you in a few minutes."

"See you in a few minutes, then." He grinned and we both headed back down the hallway. He stopped by his bedroom door, and I kept going. I could feel the nerves in my stomach as I made it into my bedroom.

"*Fuck, fuck, fuck,*" I cursed under my breath as I closed the door behind me. Why had I agreed to his idea? Why, oh, why hadn't I shot him down? I knew that he'd goaded me into his plan. But I'd show him. I would fall asleep and not even realize he was in the bed next to me. I quickly grabbed a pair of panties and my bra. Then I looked for some pajama pants and a t-shirt. I normally slept in a top and panties, with no bra, but there was no way I was going to sleep with Wade like that. That was just asking for trouble. I grabbed my hairbrush, combed it through my hair, and put some lotion on my face, then I stared at my reflection in the mirror. My cheeks were flushed a deep pink, and I looked as plain as could be. I quickly hurried into the bathroom and added a light touch of mascara and some lip gloss. I tried not to think about the fact that I wanted to look pretty for Wade.

"At least you're not sexing yourself up, Savannah." Lecturing myself was an old habit. It came with the territory of being an only child. I looked pretty but covered up. No way he would look at me in my light grey t-shirt that I'd gotten at Yosemite National park and navy flannel bottoms and think I was interested in him in any way, which was just as I wanted it. I headed towards the door, turned the light off, and made my way back to Wade's room.

"Hello?" I poked my head into the room and saw that he was sitting atop the bed, his back leaning into his giant headboard. Wade had a king-sized bed and I smiled to myself. This was going to be easy. His bed was so big that I could pretend that I was sleeping alone.

"Come on in." He waved me in. "You can close the door."

"Okay." I closed it and then walked over to him. Despite my bravado, I was starting to feel a little nervous. I made my way to the right side of the mattress and sat on it gingerly. "Shall I set my alarm and turn the lights off?"

"If you want." He shifted closer to me. "I can wake you up if you want. I wake up naturally."

"Oh, no, that's okay."

"Do you want to swim with me tomorrow morning?"

"I can't. I have to make breakfast."

"You can make it after your swim."

"But then your breakfast will be late."

"I can make allowances."

"No need, but thanks." I shifted my whole body onto the bed and ran my fingers through my hair. "I'll skip the pool for now."

"Fine." He said as he rolled onto his side. "Do I intimidate you?"

"No, why?"

"Because you're in bed wearing a bra and pajama pants, and I distinctly remember that this morning you had on no bra and no pants."

"I was under the covers." I frowned. "How would you know if I had pants on or not."

"Trust me, I always know."

"Well, I didn't want to make you uncomfortable." I licked my lips. "Frankly, I don't really care how I sleep."

"Then go ahead. It won't bother me." He smiled as he moved to get off of the bed. "Unless it makes you nervous."

"Not at all." I jumped off of the bed as well and

unclasped my bra and pulled it out through the armhole of my top. I quickly pulled my bottoms off and dropped both items onto the ground. "See?" I stood there, holding my arms against my sides so that my top didn't ride up and show off my distinctly unsexy underwear.

"You can get back on the bed." Wade moved to the side of the room and switched a light switch before heading back to the bed. "Do you want to get under the sheets or lie on top of them for now?"

"I don't mind." I got onto the bed, my t-shirt riding up over my ass as I lay back. Wade's eyes fell to my legs and I could feel a heat rising through me.

"Okay." He got back onto the bed and moved over to me. "So, we were talking about books earlier. What's your favorite book?" He leaned onto his elbow and stared at me, and I almost felt like he really cared about my answer.

"Isn't it late? Shouldn't we go to sleep?"

"I'm not particularly tired yet, are you?"

"Well, not really," I admitted. "I guess we can talk for a few minutes."

"Good." He shifted closer to me, and I swallowed hard. What the hell had I agreed to? "So, what's your favorite book?"

"Of all time?" I asked him, trying to concentrate as I felt his leg touch mine briefly.

"Yeah."

"Well, I really love this book called *Homecoming* by Cynthia Voight. I read it as a kid, and it has always stuck with me. It's about this mom that leaves her kids in a car in a grocery store parking lot and disappears, and they have to make it across the country by themselves to their grandma's house." I paused as I realized he was staring at me with an intensity on his face that surprised me. "It was really heartfelt and good."

"It sounds sad."

"The premise was sad, but it actually turned out to be a really uplifting book. What's your favorite book?"

"I don't really do favorites."

"You must have one that's really stuck with you."

"I guess *Beloved* by Toni Morrison." He laughed. "I had to read it for a college English class. It surprised me."

"I've heard of that book. I haven't read it, though. It sounds good."

"It was really good. It felt almost gothic, in a way. It was a sad, creepy, deeply personal read." He shrugged. "Not personal for me, you understand, but personal for the protagonist. It really made me realize what different experiences we all go through. We all have different hardships and obstacles to face."

"Yeah, that's true. We really do." I nodded, though I thought to myself. *How hard could he have had it?* He was a rich, hot, white male. If anyone had it made, it would be him.

"I know what you're thinking." He chuckled.

"Oh?"

"You're thinking how hard could I have had it as an upper-class white male?" He smiled and nodded as he spoke. "And you're right, of course, there are many struggles I haven't had to face, but there are other challenges I have faced that have shaped me, that have hurt me, that have made me who I am. Though I don't know if that's PC of me to say."

"I prefer honesty to political correctness." I scratched an itch in my leg and thought for a few moments. "We're in an odd time right now," I spoke slowly, pondering my words. "I'm a firm believer in everyone being compassionate and caring to others. And I do believe that certain groups of people have had it a lot harder. That doesn't dismiss the pain or struggles anyone else has faced, though. We're all in this together at the end of the day."

"I try to treat everyone as I would want to be treated." He smiled. "You're a wise woman for someone so young."

"I'm not so young. I guess my generation is at the forefront of change, that's all."

"Our conversation got deep quickly, didn't it?" He ran his hand through his hair and blinked. I could see that he was thinking about something, but I couldn't tell what. This man puzzled and intrigued me. "Did you know that when I was young, I used to think I wanted to be a writer?"

"Oh, really?" I looked at him in surprise. "What did you want to write?"

"Fantasy books, like *Lord of the Rings*." He laughed. "I was terrible, though. I used to fall asleep rereading my own chapters. They were dreadfully boring."

"Dreadfully boring?" I laughed. "You have these little English sayings sometimes, it's funny."

"I think I told you we went to boarding school in England?" He tapped the end of my nose. "I guess I picked up a lot of sayings there."

"Oh yes, you did tell me that." I was feeling almost breathless now. "How was it?"

"It was lonely at first." He shrugged. "No one I grew up with went to boarding school." His fingers now touched the side of my face. "But I grew to love it. I had a close-knit group of friends, and we spent a lot of time together. They became like second brothers."

"Was Henry there as well?"

"Yes," He nodded. "He was there and made it easier. We're only two years apart, so we're very close. He's my best friend."

"He's very handsome."

"Thank you." He grinned.

"Why are you thanking me?"

"If you think he's handsome, then you must think I'm absolutely gorgeous."

I laughed. "But you both look quite similar."

"So you do think that I'm handsome."

"You tricked me."

"Not really." His hand rested on my shoulder. "You're different than I thought you would be."

"Oh? What did you think I'd be like?"

"I don't know exactly. Maybe not so open, and not so sweet." He stroked my shoulder and groaned slightly. "This is highly inappropriate, isn't it?" He grimaced. "I shouldn't have bet you."

"It's fine." I yawned. "Oops, sorry. I'm more tired than I thought."

"Then you should get some sleep." He pulled the sheets down, and I scrambled under the covers and lay on my back. After a few seconds, I turned on my side, my back to him. Within a minute, I felt him sliding up next to me, his arm around my waist.

"What ... what are you doing?" I mumbled as he spooned me.

"I'm getting comfy."

"But you just said this was inappropriate."

"Yeah, so?" he whispered in my ear. "I said I shouldn't have bet you, but I did." He blew into my ear lightly. "Try not to get too wet."

I gasped at his comment, but he just chuckled as he pulled me closer and began to stroke my shoulder, back, and waist. I shivered a little as I felt something hard pressing against my ass and held my breath for what felt like hours as he caressed me, never moving away from the fabric of my t-shirt until I was aching to feel his fingers on my bare skin. I would never have admitted it to him, but I was starting to feel very turned on. I turned around to face him.

"Wrong move, Carter," he teased me. He pushed one of his legs through mine so that our legs were crisscrossed over each other and his thigh was close to my increasingly wet panties. I shifted my position so that he would have less access but in doing so found my face closer to his. His arm nestled on my hip bone and his lips came dangerously close towards mine.

"You're beautiful."

He kissed me lightly on the lips. I didn't want to kiss him back but as he pulled me closer to him, I couldn't stop myself. His hand moved to my neck and his fingers tugged on the slightly damp threads of hair as he deepened the kiss. Unable to resist any longer, I kissed him back, parting my lips to allow his tongue entry. He groaned as his tongue entered, and I kissed him back passionately, pushing my breasts against his chest as his fingers ran up and down my back.

I moaned in response as he nudged my legs open, and he slid his thigh all the way up so that it was pressed against my panties. I reached my fingers up to this hair, loving the silky feel of it against my fingers. I didn't care that he was my boss. I didn't care that we'd only recently met. I didn't care that he'd bet me I couldn't resist him. All my good intentions had gone out of the window. And I didn't even blame myself. Wade Hart was gorgeous and sexy and captivating, and it would take a stronger woman than me to resist him. And why should I resist him? I was ready to have some fun, and so much the better if it was with a man as hot as Wade.

"You're so sexy," he groaned against my lips as his fingers slid up the back of my t-shirt and touched the skin at my waist. I arched my back at his touch, my heart thudding as his fingers moved to the front and lightly stroked my breasts.

I shifted once more as I felt his fingers on my nipples and couldn't suppress a gasp of longing as he squeezed them. I pulled on his hair as he kissed down my neck and I didn't resist when he pulled my top off and threw it onto the ground.

"Now we're both topless," he whispered with a chuckle. He rolled me onto my back and moved on top of me. His mouth fell to my breasts, and I cried out as he took one of my nipples between his lips and suckled it. I closed my eyes, reveling in the sensation, and rubbed his back. His left hand ran up and down my stomach, his fingers inching their way to my panties as he kissed back up my neck to my lips. He shifted his position so that I could feel his erection on my stomach. He rubbed it back and forth against me. Half-consciously, I parted my legs as his tongue once again entered my mouth, and I reached down to touch the front of his cock. I giggled slightly as it twitched against my hand, and Wade groaned as I slipped a finger into his boxers to touch him, skin to skin. He kissed the side of my neck, and I felt his fingers moving further downward, slip-ping into my panties where they paused for a moment. Blood roared in my ears as he sucked on my skin, and just as I was on the verge of begging, his fingers slipped down further and rubbed against me gently. Trembling with desire, I opened my legs a bit more so that I could feel more of him against me. Two fingers rubbed me more urgently and a deep feeling of want for more spread through me. I was about to pull down his boxers when he chuckled slightly.

"What's so funny?" I said, my eyes fluttering open to look at him as he gazed at me. He pulled his fingers out of my panties and rubbed them against my stomach.

"Just how wet you are." He winked at me as he reached his fingers up to his mouth and sucked on them. "I can taste your juices, Savannah, so sweet and horny, just like you." He kissed my lips, and I pushed him off of me.

"You're an asshole." I glared at him, my body trying to keep up with my brain.

"No, I'm just a sexy piece of meat." He laughed as he rolled over onto his side. His fingers idly played with my breasts and he pulled me close. "I guess you already know that you lost the bet."

"Whatever."

"So that means no additional $5000 for you."

"Okay."

"But we forgot to state what my prize was if I won."

"Your prize?" I shook my head. "Your prize was having me here in the first place."

"Was it?" His hand slid from my breasts back down towards my panties, but this time they rubbed over the top of the material. I tried to stifle a moan as he rubbed my clit. Part of me wanted to tell him to stop, but it just felt too good. I was embarrassed that I was loving the way that he was making me feel. "You can choose my prize. So I want either: one, both of us to sleep naked tonight, or two, you share the bed with me again tomorrow night and you can wear what you want."

"I'm not sleeping naked with you."

"We're both pretty close to naked right now."

"Close isn't the same as actually naked, though." I couldn't imagine what would happen if we were both naked. Actually, I could imagine, and while I did want to have sex, I didn't want to have sex right now and with him.

"So, we sleep together tomorrow night, then?"

"Fine," I mumbled. I sounded pissed, though inside I was quite excited by the possibility of spending another night with him.

"I'll let you fall asleep now. You have an early morning

tomorrow." He kissed me on the forehead and rolled over. "Sweet dreams, Savannah."

Why had he stopped so suddenly? Confused, I turned over onto my side and closed my eyes and willed myself to drift off to sleep. A moment later, he tucked me up against himself, spooning me again. This time his hand lay on my bare stomach as his hardness pushed up against my ass. I didn't even bother trying to move, even though I was feeling hornier than ever, with him pressed up against me.

"You were right not to choose us sleeping naked together," Wade whispered in my ear as he kissed the back of my head.

"Oh?" I murmured back to him.

"If we were naked right now, my cock would be nestled warmly in your pussy or your ass." He chuckled as his hand slid up to my breast and he held me close. "And I'm not sure you walking funny because I slammed the hell out of your pussy with my massive cock would be the best way to start your third day at work."

He laughed. My panties got even wetter, but I kept my lips firmly closed, refusing to respond to his comment even as excitement coursed through me. Maybe there had been more to his job advertisement after all. And maybe I'd be quite okay with finding out exactly what that was.

"Also," he whispered into the room. "I wouldn't want your boyfriend to get jealous either."

I froze at his words and stifled in a sigh. Shit, not only did Wade think I was a slut and a tease, he most probably thought I was a cheater as well.

CHAPTER 11

I woke up, relieved to find myself alone in Wade's bed.

"Oh, man," I grumbled, making a face as I picked my t-shirt up from the floor and slipped it on. I grabbed my pajama bottoms and hurried out of the bedroom. As I made my way along the corridor, I thought about the previous night and how I'd let Wade touch me. My cheeks heated up as I thought about the way he'd played with my nipples as we'd drifted off to sleep. I couldn't believe I'd let him do that. And tonight, I was supposed to sleep with him again. Only tonight, I would stop him if he tried to do more than kiss me. Yes, I would let him kiss me again, but I wouldn't let him go any further than that. No, his hands would have to stay to themselves.

I knew that was easier said than done, though.

I hurried to shower and change and then made my way to the kitchen in my maid's outfit so that I could make his breakfast made for him. I felt like a bit of a fool as I whisked eggs for an omelet. When I'd gone to college, I'd never imagined that I'd end up with a job like this, but then again, most of my graduating class was probably in jobs they never expected to be in. That was just how the economy was going right now.

"Well, good morning, Savannah. How are you today?" said a warm voice. I looked around to see Henry standing there with a box in his hands. "I brought some doughnuts. I hope you don't mind if I join you for breakfast?"

"Not at all. Have a seat. I love doughnuts." I took the offered box from him and opened it up to peek inside. "Wow, these smell fresh."

"They should still be warm as well." He grinned. "I got some glazed and jelly ones. Do you have any fresh coffee? Maybe I'll have one now."

"Ooh, I just put the pot on. I would love to have a hot doughnut as well." I beamed at him. "You've made my morning."

"I'm glad to help." His eyes moved back and forth over my uniform and he raised an eyebrow at me. "I like the outfit."

"Do you really?" I shook my head. "I feel like a fool. Your brother ..." I let my voice trail off, unsure how to continue. I'd just gotten out of his brother's bed. I'd spent the night making out with Wade, sleeping half-naked. His fingers had touched me in my most intimate place, and I had wanted more. I couldn't tell Henry how confused I was about everything that was going on. How could I? He'd think I was crazy.

"I bet I know what you're going to say." Henry laughed and took a bite out of the doughnut he'd just taken from the box. "You're going to say that my brother is an ass and a jerk and thinks far too highly of himself." I allowed myself one quick nod. "I'm surprised you wore this outfit."

"It's not an outfit, it's my uniform."

"Is it really? That's the uniform of an assistant to a billionaire?"

"I don't know." I pursed my lips. "Well, I mean, I do know. It's demeaning as hell, but what can I say? He's my boss, he makes the rules, not me."

"And you just go along with them?" He looked thoughtful for a moment. "Maybe I won't be getting my Ferrari after all."

"Sorry, what?" I grabbed the whistling kettle and poured the hot water onto the freshly ground coffee beans in the French press. "Would you like milk and sugar with your coffee? Or do you prefer it black?"

"I prefer it black, but thanks for asking." He sat back down and I could tell from his expression that he was thinking about something. "Savannah, I want to tell you that I think you're a very strong woman, an intelligent one as well. You shouldn't allow my brother to intimidate you—"

"Are you saying I intimidate her?" Wade strode into the kitchen, body dripping with water and a frown on his face. "Good morning, brother of mine. Morning, Savannah." He strode over to me and smiled. "Sleep well, did you?"

"I slept okay." I shrugged as my eyes fell to his wet, muscular chest. How I wished I'd run my fingers over those abs last night. I'd have to make sure to touch them tonight just to see how they felt.

"Good." He smiled and leaned down to whisper in my ear. "Did you know you snore when you sleep?"

"No." I blushed and glanced over to Henry who was now staring at us with unconcealed curiosity in his light green eyes. He looked so much like Wade as he sat there, but there was something more boyish about him, something gentler that made him seem more approachable and fun-loving.

Unlike Wade, who was now standing there, staring at me with a veiled look of lust in his eyes. Wade was all man. There was nothing boyish about his looks, personality, or attitude. Henry was the sort of guy that would ask if it were okay to toss you onto your back and kiss you; Wade was the sort of man who'd just do it. I shivered as Wade touched my arm. His fingers were slightly cold.

"How much longer until breakfast is ready? I'm ready to eat." He grinned. "Whatever you're offering." He winked at me as he glanced down towards my legs. I gasped at the insinuation in his tone. "You okay?" He tilted his head to the side, a teasing smile on his handsome face.

"Your fingers were cold and you're still wet," I mumbled.

"I bet I'm not the only one that's wet right now," he said under his breath so that only he and I could hear him. I blushed bright red.

"What's going on?" Henry stood up and approached us. "And, brother? Why do you have Savannah wearing this ridiculous get up?"

"Because I can." Wade sounded smug. "Why do you care?"

"Maybe because I have a vested interest in Savannah's work here." Henry shot back at his brother. I frowned, confused. What vested interest did he have?

"She's not single, you know, brother." Wade chuckled. "She has a boyfriend, and who knows what else going on."

"Well about that ..." I bit down on my lower lip, feeling awkward. "We, uh, we broke up."

"You broke up?" Wade turned to me with a raised eyebrow. "Really?"

"Really." I nodded. "It wasn't going to work out."

"So, between late last night and this morning, you broke up?" Wade smirked. "Interesting."

"It was already getting bad," I lied, wanting to change the subject.

"Must have been." He arched one eyebrow. "Shit, if my lips and fingers can cause an immediate breakup, who knows what other parts of me can do."

"It had nothing to do with you!" I snapped. Both he and Henry looked at me with surprised smiles.

"What the hell has gone on between you two?" Henry looked at Wade. "I know you work fast, brother, but really? Two nights with your new assistant and you're already making moves?"

"He's not making any moves," I said quickly, embarrassed. "Now are you guys hungry or not?" I grabbed some plates and quickly moved them to the table. "Have a seat, and I will serve you both."

"Yes, dear." Henry shook his head and laughed as he headed back to the table. "Wade, it seems to me that you found your perfect woman."

"Perhaps." Wade looked at me with narrowed eyes and took a seat. I glared at him and turned around so that I could grab the pan with the omelet. "I think you just got a text." Wade held up my phone, which had been resting on the table.

"Okay, must be Lucy." She was the only one who would be texting me before nine in the morning.

"No," Wade's voice sounded dry. "It looks like it's a Gordon. And he wants to know if you have any plans for tonight."

"Oh."

"Is that one of your friends in the City?" Wade said, his voice sounding irritated. "Shall I tell him you've moved?"

"He's not a friend in the city." I shook my head as I approached the table. "He's actually a man I met last night. A very nice man. He's an actor." I placed the dishes on the table. "Help yourselves, boys."

"A man you met last night?" Henry grinned. "You work fast, Savannah."

"I don't." I blushed. "He just ended up sitting next to me."

"Is he the reason you dumped your boyfriend?" Henry looked happy as he grabbed a piece of toast. "And here Wade was thinking it was because of him, but it's because you've gone and met yourself a new guy."

Wade shot a dark glance at his brother then looked back at me. "You do seem to flit from man to man, don't you, Savannah?" He sounded angry. "Are you going to tell Gordon about last night?"

"No." I glared at him, and Henry's eyes widened.

"Oh, shit, what happened last night?" He looked back and forth between me and his brother. "Don't tell me you guys fu— I mean made love." He cleared his throat. I could tell he was trying not to laugh.

"No, of course not." I shook my head quickly as Wade just sat there staring at me. "We just had a little bet, that's all, and I shared his bed."

"Well, that's not really all, is it, Savannah?" Wade grabbed a piece of bacon. "You slept in a pair of panties and a short t-shirt, with no bra. Not exactly the most conservative of attire."

"But you—" I realized he was deliberately trying to get a rise out of me. "If I recall correctly, you were the one trying to make moves on me. I was just trying to sleep." I shrugged casually. "Pass my phone, please, I don't want to leave Gordon hanging. What time will I be off tonight?"

"Tonight?" Wade raised an eyebrow. "Oh, didn't I tell you? I thought you could make a nice dinner tonight. Henry will join, won't you?" He looked at his brother who was still grinning from ear to ear. "Have it ready for 7 p.m., and set the table for three."

"So I'm to eat dinner at home tonight, is that what you're saying?"

"I'm saying you are making dinner for three tonight." Wade shrugged. "And I'm assuming it will be a three to five-course meal, so it should last several hours." He bit into a piece of bread. "But of course, if you have some sort of booty call with Gordon tonight, I guess you can fit him in. Don't forget our arrangement for the night, though."

"I do not have a booty call arrangement with Gordon." I grabbed my phone from him, trying to hide my fury. "And even if I did, it's none of your business."

"As you say." He shrugged. "It's none of my concern. Just make sure to cook a nice meal for tonight." He suddenly pulled back his chair and stood up. "I need to go and shower, and then I have a call." His expression was blank, and I had no idea what he was thinking about. "Go to the library and start work at around 10 a.m. I'll place a stack of files on the desk and I'll send you an email about some tasks I need done. Then you can go to the village later to pick up some groceries. Henry, give her the keys to the Range Rover and show her where to put the gas and all that." He pushed his chair under the table. "You can drive into town yourself. I take it you have a phone with Google Maps on it so you don't get lost?"

"Yes."

"Good." And with that he was gone, striding out of the kitchen and not looking back.

"Well, I must say, you and my brother have some real chemistry going on, don't you?" Henry looked surprised. "I've haven't seen him this irritated in a while."

"He's a jerk."

"Yet you like him." He smiled at me gently. "That's why you're putting up with it, isn't it?"

"No!" I protested quickly. "I just met him. I need the money. That's the only reason why."

"He'd like to think that." Henry shook his head. "But I'm pretty sure I know differently. Well, tonight will be fun, won't it? A regular little dinner party for the three of us to get to know each other better."

"What does that mean?"

Henry laughed. "Oh, Savannah, if looks could kill." He took another bite of toast. "My brother might be crazy and I might be a flirt, but we're not kinky. Well, at least not *that* kinky. I don't mind having a threesome, but not with my brother." He made a face. "Definitely never with my brother, and if I'm honest, not with another man. I prefer my threesomes to be of the two-women variety." He laughed as I blushed. "You are quite innocent, aren't you?"

"No, no, I'm not." I looked down and ate a piece of omelet. "I just want to ensure you know I'm not interested in any group sex activities or anything. I know that I took this job and came up here as if I were some sort of desperado, but I'm not. My best friend, Lucy knows I'm here, and she's willing to come up at any time to bring me home."

"She sounds like a good best friend."

"She's the best."

"Well, that's good, then." Henry sat back. "I have a feeling you'll be needing someone to vent to very soon." He continued eating.

I just kept my mouth shut because I wanted and needed to do a lot more than vent right now.

CHAPTER 12

"Hey, Savannah, I know you might have planned the menu already, but I had some special requests." Wade strode into the library and took a seat at the table next to me. "First off, I'd like to start with some mini quiches and maybe a shrimp cocktail."

"Uhm, okay." I closed the laptop. "Let me write this down."

I grabbed a pen and my yellow legal pad and looked at my current menu. It consisted of tomato soup, garlic bread, devilled eggs, and spaghetti. I scratched those items off and wrote down his suggestions, feigning indifference to the requests. How the hell was I going to make mini quiches? I didn't even know how to make proper-sized quiches.

"Anything else?"

"I was hoping you'd be able to make a beef Wellington for the main dish. And maybe a blueberry pie for dessert? Or a peach cobbler, as you're from the South."

"Well, we don't really consider ourselves as being from the South."

"But Florida is in the South."

"Yes, but we're not Southern. Not like people from Alabama or Georgia or—"

"Is this your way of telling me you don't know how to make a peach cobbler?"

"This is my way of telling you I don't know how to make shit," I mumbled, covering the words with a cough.

"Sorry, I didn't understand what you said."

He peered at me expectantly, and I couldn't help admiring his handsome features. I wanted to run my hands through his hair and stroke his beard and lean in and kiss him. But that wasn't the type of relationship we had. Not that we had a relationship at all. He was my boss and maybe a possible hookup. He wasn't my boyfriend.

"Also, tell me more about what happened between you and your boyfriend?" he continued. "It didn't have to do with what happened last night, did it?" He smirked. "I have been told that I have the lips of a sex god, and you seemed to be dying for us to—"

"It had nothing to do with you," I cut him off. He really was the most egotistical man I'd ever met.

"Oh, yeah?" He laughed and then shook his head. "Savannah, I'm not sure what game you're playing, but I know you didn't have a boyfriend."

"Excuse me? Are you saying that I lied?"

"Yes." He walked over to a stack of books and pulled down a red leather photo album and brought it back to the table. "You're too much of a romantic, too sweet, and I believe—though not in this instance—too honest." He opened one of the photo albums and flipped through it. "There's no way you would have gotten into bed and kissed me if you were in a relationship."

"That is true," I finally admitted. "I wasn't exactly in a relationship."

"So, you're admitting you didn't have a boyfriend?"

"Maybe."

"I knew it." His eyes were gleeful. "Your reaction to me last night was that of a woman who hadn't been touched in a while."

"What does that mean?"

"Do you really want to know?"

"Yes." I blushed.

"Well, and I don't mean to be crude ..." He laughed. "Who am I kidding? I don't care. Let's just say, when I slid my fingers into your panties, you were wetter than a Slip 'n' Slide." He winked at me. "I'm pretty sure you were feeling horny from the moment my lips touched yours. And those little moans you gave." He licked his lips. "You were enjoying the moment far too much for someone who would also have guilty feelings if she were cheating."

"I … see."

What could I say in response to that? He was correct, of course. I'd loved the feel of his fingers on me, his tongue had felt like silk, and my entire body had wanted to feel him inside of me. Not that I was going to admit that.

"I'm glad to hear I was right," he said with a self-satisfied smile. "Here, have a look at this." He pushed the photo album toward me. "This is a photo of Henry and me as kids." He pointed to a photo of two young boys with blond hair. To the right of them, their dad stood beaming next to a barbeque. "This photo was taken the day before my sixth birthday. You might think my mother took the photo. She didn't. She was in Palm Beach at a golf fundraiser with actresses and politicians." He looked into my eyes. "This is the reality of relationships, Savannah. Smoke and mirrors. Photos lie. People lie."

I recoiled from him, upset at his tone. "Why are you telling me this?"

"Because I don't want you thinking that the world is this

magical place and love makes it all go around. You're young, maybe a bit naive. I'm not trying to dash your hopes, but you're not just going to move to a small town, go to a bar, and meet the man of your dreams."

"I never said I was going to meet the man of my dreams." I squeezed the pen in my fingers. "What are you talking about?"

"I'm just saying life isn't a fairytale, and you're not some princess about to be rescued by your Prince Charming."

"Wade, I don't know what high horse you're on, but you need to jump on down. I don't need you to school me on anything. And while I'm sorry for your parents and their marriage, that doesn't mean true love doesn't exist."

He snorted. "Ask yourself how much you really could have liked that guy if you still slept with me."

"I didn't sleep with you." I rolled my eyes. "And Gordon has nothing to do with you."

"Defending him already?"

"Wade, do you have any other information you want to share about dinner tonight?" I took a deep breath. "Also, is it a dress-up event?"

"Yes."

"So I should dress up?"

"You should dress appropriately, yes." He cleared his throat. "As to the menu, you can make some of your specials." He stood up. "I think you should go into town and get the ingredients now, and when you get back, you can start cooking."

"Okay." I pressed my lips together to stop myself from saying anything else. I was going to have to look up some more recipes. "Is that all?"

"You sound like you want me to leave."

"Maybe that's because I do."

"Really?" He smiled. "I'm looking forward to tonight."

"I bet you are."

"Aren't you?"

"Seeing as you enjoy my honesty, I'm going to be honest. No."

"Liar." He grinned and headed towards the door. "The Range Rover is in the driveway, and the keys are on the table. You can drive, right?"

"Yes, Wade. I can drive." I stood up as well. "I also emailed you the mockup of the database you wanted. And a preliminary list of non-profits. I will get started on some marketing materials later today."

"I don't think you'll have time today, Savannah, but tomorrow will be fine." He stopped by the doorway and smiled warmly at me. "You're doing a good job, thank you."

"A good job in the bedroom or out?" I quipped back. I was teasing, but I immediately regret my words.

"Which one are you hoping to do a good job in?" He gave me a lazy wink and left the room.

I stood there staring at the empty doorway and then buried my face in my hands. This was a hot mess. In fact, this was a fiery volcanic mess. Wade was on a different playing field from me, and I wasn't able to keep up. I grabbed my phone and purse and made a beeline for the back door. I'd look up the recipes on my phone. I just needed to get out of this house and try to figure out what was going on.

"One second, Savannah, I'm just leaving the office to get a coffee." Lucy answered the phone as I drove out of the Hart estate and made my way into town.

"Okay." Fortunately, the car was connected by Bluetooth, so I could talk and drive at the same time. I drove down the driveway, feeling lighter. The car was luxurious, and it was a bright sunny day. Maybe if I shopped quickly, I could get a coffee in town and just sit back for a half an hour or so.

"Hey, I'm back." Lucy sounded breathless. "Sorry. Everything in the office is just getting crazy. The market's not great, so we're not making a lot of money, and people are stressed out."

"Oh, no, are you okay?"

"I'm fine. I miss you though."

"I miss you, too."

"So, what are you up to?"

"I'm driving to the village right now to go shopping for dinner. Wade is having a dinner party for me, him, and his brother, and he wants me to cook up all his favorite dishes."

"Oh, shit, Savannah, you're not exactly Julia Child." Lucy sounded worried. "How's that going to work?"

"I know how to follow recipes, it should be okay." I tried to sound convincing.

"Girl, I'm your best friend. I've seen you burn frozen pizza and set off the fire alarm boiling eggs." Lucy giggled. "What does Wade want you to cook?"

"Mini quiches and shrimp cocktail."

"Mini quiches." Lucy started laughing harder now. "I'm sorry, Savannah, but really? Oh, my God, what are you going to do?"

"Well, if you want me to be one hundred percent honest, there's a bakery in town, and I'm going to see if they have any." I laughed. "And shrimp cocktail looks easy. I just boil up some shrimp and put some cocktail sauce in a dish. Easy peasy. Even I can't mess that up."

"Boil the shrimp?" Lucy sounded uncertain. "I think you should sauté them."

"Maybe I'll sauté them with some garlic. That sounds good."

"I'm not sure about the garlic for a shrimp cocktail."

"Oh." I sighed. "This sucks."

"Yeah, it's crazy that he expects you to be his cook as well."

"I agree ..." My voice trailed off. "So ... I went to that poetry slam last night, well, it wasn't a poetry slam, but an open mic night. You know what I mean."

"How was it?"

"It was good, I met this cool guy. Oh, and I also made out with Wade last night. In his bed."

"You *what*?" Lucy shouted. "Shit, I need to lower my voice, two guys just looked over at me. What is going on? You met a guy, and you made out with Wade? We're talking Wade, your asshole boss?"

"Yes, I'm talking Wade, my asshole boss." I bit my lip. "It was kinda nice, if I'm honest."

"Okay, how did that happen?"

"It just kinda happened, but let's just say we did more than kiss."

"Oh, my God, do not tell me you gave it up to him?"

"No, of course not."

"So? What else did you do?"

"Let's just say my top was off and his top was off."

"Okay." She giggled. "We sound like high school girls, you know that, right?"

"Just a little bit." I paused. "He has a huge cock."

"Well, that's not high school. How do you know? Did you blow him?"

"No, but I felt it against me, and my fingers grazed it. I wanted to blow him, though." I laughed. "I was horny as hell."

"I thought you hated him?"

"I do hate him. That doesn't mean I can't also be super turned on by him."

"Wow, I need to meet this guy. He must be hot."

"He is *super* hot," I said a little dreamily then snapped back to reality. "I think he has issues, though. His mom was a deadbeat and basically ditched him and his brother. I don't think he believes in love."

"Ugh, that's bad, but are you looking to marry the guy? Have some fun while you're up there and then come home." Lucy laughed. "Hit it and quit it, girl."

"You make losing my virginity sound so romantic."

"Obviously, you don't *want* that. Ideally, you'd meet the man of your dreams and fall in love and make love on the beach or whatever, but girl, we don't meet men like that."

"That's because men like that don't exist outside of the Hallmark Channel."

"Exactly. I'm not saying to do it with Wade. I'm saying to be open to the experience."

"Are you meeting any guys you can be open to?" I asked, hoping Lucy had also met someone.

"Does the guy that bags the groceries at the store count?" She laughed. "He asked me for my number yesterday."

"Oooh, he did?"

"Why do you sound excited, Savannah? I'm not dating the eighty-year-old man from the grocery store. Shit, he's even too old for my grandma, and she's in her late sixties."

"Oh, Lucy, ha ha, I miss you."

"I miss you too, though your life is sounding super exciting right now. Who knew that a job in the country was all you needed to jumpstart your love life?"

"Well, I wouldn't exactly say it jump started my love life. My love life is still pretty dead."

"So, who is this other guy you met last night? Is he a potential as well?"

"He seemed nice, very friendly, very sweet. Though, I don't think we're a match."

"Oh, why not?"

"I think he might be gay." I laughed.

"Are you sure?"

"No … but he's an actor, and he was well-dressed, and I just got that vibe."

"Oh, Savannah." Lucy laughed. "Not a potential love match, then?"

"No, I'm pretty sure he's not. A new friend though, which is perfect because I need some friends up here. He actually texted me this morning about hanging out tonight."

"And you're sure he's not straight?"

"I don't know for sure," I admitted. "But even though he's handsome, he's no comparison to Wade."

"Wow, you're really into Wade. I guess it's always the obnoxious ones that get the girls."

"It's hard to explain, Lucy. A part of me is so infuriated by him, but then another part of me just wants to kiss him and touch him. He's such an enigma. He can be sweet and caring and teasing, and then other times, he seems like this bitter asshole." I glanced at the GPS navigator and made a left turn onto the road that was to take me to the main shopping street in the village. "And he's so sexy." I shook my head even though Savannah couldn't see me. "The man could melt ice cream just by looking at it."

"Oh, Savannah, you've got it bad."

"I don't have it bad, I just think there's a lot more to him than meets the eye. And, well … maybe I want to unpeel his layers."

"You want to unpeel his layers all right. You want him naked." Lucy and I both started laughing. "You want to suck on that lollipop."

"Girl, it's much bigger than a lollipop." I passed a sign letting me know I was close to Herne Hill Village. "And maybe tonight I'll get a lick." I groaned. "Oh, Lucy, what are you doing to me? Let me concentrate on the road, and I'll let you get back to work. I'll talk to you later."

"Have a good night, Savannah. I hope the dinner goes well. And stay safe. And practice safe sex if you decide that Wade is the right guy." Lucy took a deep breath. "I hope it all goes as you want it to."

"Thanks, girl. I'll call you tomorrow."

As I hung up the phone I thought about her last words, *I hope it all goes as you want it to.* What did I really want? If I just focused on me and not on Wade, what did I want from this situation? What did I want from Wade? Did I want him to be my first? Did I want to just go with the flow, and then when my contract was up, leave and continue on in my life? And could I even do that? Could I sleep with this man and just leave? And what if I fell for him? What if I wanted more? How would he feel? He'd made it clear he didn't believe in true love.

I sighed. Maybe the moral of the story was that I just needed to wait. Maybe I should have no expectations. I hadn't even known even him a week, after all. What was to be would be.

🌻

"Everything is looking and smelling delicious, Savannah." Wade walked into the kitchen wearing a dark suit and crisp white shirt. His hair was freshly washed, and he'd trimmed his moustache and beard. He had an air of excitement about him, and I couldn't help but smile as he walked toward me. "Shall I open a bottle of wine?" he asked.

"Sure, that would be great."

"Will you have time to change before dinner starts?" He peered at me as if he were gazing into my soul and I nodded quickly, looking away and focusing on buttering the French bread I was about to heat in the oven. "I'll set the table to save you time."

"Will we be eating in here?" I nodded over to the kitchen table.

"We won't be, no." He shook his head. "I'll get the nice silver and china plates and place them on the dining room table."

"Wow, sounds fancy." I grinned.

"Just a little." He moved closer to me and looked down into my eyes. "You have the most open eyes." His nose brushed mine as he lightly kissed me. "When I look at you, I can read your every emotion."

"Well, that doesn't sound good." I was breathless. "When I look into your eyes, I can't tell anything you're thinking."

"I'm good at hiding my feelings. You have to be when you're in business."

"I suppose that's true." I kissed him back lightly, and his eyes widened in surprise. "What?"

"I didn't expect you to kiss me back."

"Why not?"

"You seem shy."

"I might be a little shy, but you kissed me first." I shrugged. "I figured it was okay to kiss you back."

"I suppose it was okay, it just surprised me." He looked hesitant. "You don't hate me, do you?"

"Why would I hate you?" I blinked at him. It was my turn to be surprised.

"You said I was arrogant, a jerk, an asshole? Something along those lines, I believe." He laughed.

"Well, you are a bit of all of those things. But you're also kinda cute. And fun to kiss."

"You're fun to kiss as well."

"I know." I winked at him, and he burst out laughing.

"I'm going to enjoy tonight," he murmured as he slid a hand around my ass. "I'm going to enjoy it immensely."

"The dinner?"

"The dinner, yes, but I'm thinking that there's something else I'll enjoy more." His hand slid to my waist, and he pulled me into him. His lips fell to my neck, and he kissed me softly. "I want you, Savannah. I would be lying if I said I didn't. And I think you want me as well."

"Maybe."

"Just maybe?" His hand slid up to my breast and squeezed gently. "If I didn't have this dinner party planned, I'd be bending you over and sliding into you right now," he growled. "I'm so hard right now just thinking about being inside of you." I shivered at the lust I could see in his eyes. "I want to fuck you, Savannah."

"Is that a part of the job description?" I whispered. I stroked his face, enjoying the intensity of his expression.

"No." He grinned. "It's just a perk." He just looked at me for a few seconds before stepping back. "I should go and get everything ready. Dinner will be ready at seven?"

"Yeah." I nodded, wondering why it was so important for the dinner to start at seven. "When will Henry be here?"

"Any moment, I think." He smiled. "Okay, let me make myself busy." And he stepped away from me. I turned back to the stove to fluff the pot of rice and mixed vegetables I was cooking. I didn't have a fancy dress to put on, but I would do my best to dress nicely. I was quite excited for the evening. I almost felt like the lady of the house cooking for Wade and his brother. It was almost as if we were throwing a dinner party. I checked to make sure that everything was cooking as it should and walked down the corridor so that I could change.

"Oh, Savannah?" Wade called after me as I walked past the dining room.

"Yes, Wade?"

"Thanks for putting on your uniform tonight."

"What?"

"You're putting on your uniform, right?"

"My uniform?" I blinked. I was confused. Why would I be putting on my uniform for dinner? Oh, shit. Was this some sort of fantasy? Did Wade have a threesome planned with him and his brother? Henry had said no, but maybe he just didn't want me to know in advance.

"Yeah," Wade walked out of the dining room. "What else would you serve us in?"

"Serve you in?" I raised an eyebrow. "What do you mean?"

The doorbell rang. Wade's eyes crinkled as he looked at my angry face. "Sorry, I have to get that. Go and change, Savannah. Now." He dismissed me and headed to the door. "Scoot, Savannah. I'm getting the door, you get ready."

I stood there for a moment, stunned, then dragged myself back to my room where I put on my maid's uniform. Had I gotten it completely wrong? I crept back to the kitchen. I could hear Henry laughing at something and then the shrill laugh of a woman joining him.

There was a third guest. The table was set for three. The dinner was for three.

I wasn't there to eat dinner with Henry and Wade. I was the help there to serve them. My face burned. I'd assumed the meal was for me as well, though Wade hadn't directly said that. But he hadn't said there was someone else coming. He had deliberately let me believe I was going to be eating with him and Henry. All my warm feelings towards him vanished like smoke. Wade Hart was a jackass. I couldn't believe that I'd actually thought he was a good guy. And to think I'd even been considering going down on him tonight. No way, Jose. His cock was coming nowhere near my mouth, and I was going nowhere near his bed. He could piss off. I was going to keep everything professional from here on out. I wasn't going to be his plaything to just treat as he wanted. Jerk!

"Savannah? Savannah, can you come here for a moment, please?" Wade called me from the dining room and I walked there slowly.

"Can I help you, sir?" There was no smile on my face as I entered the room, and I knew my expression was surly.

"Yes, we'd like some wine, please." He looked over at Henry, who was just shaking his head. "Henry will have a glass of white." And then he looked over to the woman on his right, a tall redhead with creamy pale skin and large blue eyes. She looked like a delicate flower, and I tried to ignore the jealousy that rushed through me. "And you, Etta, what would you like?"

"Ooh, I'll have a glass of red, please Wade." She touched his arm lightly and batted her eyelids at him. She was wearing a tight black dress that hugged her figure in all the right places. "You know white does my head in."

"I'll join you with a glass of red." He looked over at me. "Did you get that, Savannah?"

"Yes," I mumbled. "I did."

"Did you get to tell your new friend you won't be able to make it tonight?" Wade continued. "He understands you're working, right?"

"He doesn't mind how late I am." I smiled at him sweetly. "He's ready for me at any time." Which was a lie. I hadn't even texted Gordon back as yet, but Wade didn't have to know that.

"Is there a reason why you're not getting our drinks?" Wade raised an eyebrow and I glared at him furiously as I hurried out of the room.

"I was just answering your question, asshole," I muttered under my breath as I walked into the kitchen.

Henry followed me out of the room. "Don't let him bother you," he said in a low voice.

"He's an asshole." I shook my head as I stared at him. "He's the one that asked me a question. It's not like I was just standing there."

"I know." Henry shook his head. "My brother is stupid."

"Who's the woman? His date?"

"Who is Henrietta?" He shook his head. "She's just an old friend of his."

"A bed buddy?"

"I don't know." He shook his head. "Maybe in the past. Not now."

"Really? Well, she sure looked like she wanted to get her paws into him."

"All the women want Wade." Henry laughed. "Just ignore it."

"Oh, I don't need to ignore it. I don't care."

"You know if Wade is getting on your nerves, you can walk out and tell him to stuff it, right?"

"It's fine." I shook my head. "I mean, he hasn't really done anything to me. I'm his employee."

"You thought you were going to be a dinner guest, didn't you?" Henry shook his head. "My brother is an ass."

"It's fine." I took a deep breath. "I already had a feeling that he was a jerk. I just need to remember that moving forward."

"Oh, Savannah." Henry put a hand on my shoulder. "You don't have to accept everything Wade says and does."

"I know that." I nodded, tears welling in my eyes. I turned away from Henry, embarrassed by the night's turn of events. How had Wade been flirting with me just minutes ago and now he was back to treating me like the help?

"Savannah." Henry tilted my head up to look at him. "Are you crying?"

"I'm not crying." My lower lip trembled, and a tear rolled down my cheek. Henry reached his arms around me and pulled me into his arms and hugged me.

"Ignore my brother, Savannah. He always goes too far when he's trying to prove a point. I'm sorry."

"What point is he trying to prove?" I looked up at him, and Henry looked away guiltily.

"I've said too much." He stepped back and sighed. "Just know that you can speak up, Savannah. I know you want to." He looked around the kitchen. "Now how can I be helpful? Shall I take the glasses of wine inside?"

"Do you mind?" I asked him softly, taking a deep breath. "That will give me time to get the appetizers ready."

"I don't mind at all." Henry touched my shoulder, his eyes crinkling as he smiled down at me. He looked so much like Wade in that moment that I felt my heart stop for a few seconds. "He's not as horrible as he seems. I know that's hard to believe, but trust me, somewhere deep in his heart, he's a good guy."

"I'm not convinced he actually has one." I deep breath. "But you know what, I don't care. This is just a job, and I need to remember that. I will just mark off the days on the calendar, and when my time is up, I'll be out and I won't be looking back."

"Is that so?" Wade's deep voice made me jump as he walked into the kitchen. He surveyed my face, and his lips thinned. "We'll talk later." He turned around and walked back out of the kitchen. Henry just shook his head. I took a deep breath and flattened my skirt down.

I didn't know what the hell was going on and I didn't care. I was done with Wade and his hot and cold games. I might be young and inexperienced, but I wasn't looking for heartache and drama with a man who just wanted to mess with my head—no matter how good looking he was.

I put the last dish into the dishwasher and closed the door. Finally, the night had come to an end. I'd spent the evening ignoring Wade, and I hadn't made eye contact with him once. I was ready to go to bed, and I was going to sleep in as late as I wanted. No way was I waking up early to make him breakfast. I didn't care what he expected. My stomach growled as I leaned back against the sink. I hadn't even gotten a chance to eat yet.

The meal had gone okay. The shrimp cocktail looked good, the mini quiches were frozen from a packet, and I'd bought a frozen lasagna and garlic bread and pretended I'd made them. I didn't care if Wade knew or not. I walked to the fridge to make myself a sandwich when I heard footsteps walking into the kitchen.

"You didn't have to do the dishes tonight."

"It's my job." I didn't bother turning around to face Wade.

"I'm not a slave driver."

"Can I help you?" I grabbed some cheese from the fridge and a knife from the drawer.

"I came to thank you for dinner." He walked over to me. "Still hungry?"

"Still?" I looked up at him angrily. "I haven't gotten to eat yet."

"You haven't?"

"I've spent the evening serving you and your brother and friend." I glared at him. "When did I have time to eat?"

"I guess you should eat now, then." He shrugged. "No homemade lasagna for you?"

"No." My lips thinned, and I turned away.

"What about some Stouffers, then?" There was mirth in

his voice. I willed myself not to react and confirm what he already knew.

"I'm tired, Wade, am I still on the clock?"

"No."

"Then leave me the hell alone," I burst out. "I just want to eat and go to bed."

"Wow, ready for me already, huh?"

"I'm not sleeping in your bed tonight, Wade." I shook my head. "Last night was a mistake. I'm not interested in your games." I rolled my eyes. "Why don't you call Henrietta and tell her that you need a bed buddy tonight. I'm sure she'll be happy for you to slide on in."

"Slide on in, huh?" He raised an eyebrow. "Such poetry."

"Whatever, Wade."

"Are you really this upset?" He shook his head. "Just because I had a female dinner guest?"

"You know that's not why I'm upset. You led me to believe that I was going to be the third guest at the dinner table. I thought I was cooking for the three of us."

"I'm sorry, did I say that?" He cocked his head to the side. "I didn't realize I said you'd be a guest."

"Well, you didn't say that exactly," I mumbled. "I guess I just assumed."

"So then, that was on you."

"Okay, fine. It was my fault."

"Are you upset because you didn't get to see your friend tonight?"

"Oh, my God, enough already about Gordon." I pushed past him. "I'm going to bed."

"What about the cheese?"

"*You* can put it away," I snapped.

I stormed out of the kitchen, down the corridor, and into my bedroom, slamming the door behind me. I walked into the shower, pulling my clothes off and dropping them on the bathroom floor. I stepped in and let the water pour down on me. I closed my eyes and tried to relax. As the tension seeped out of me, a poem started forming in my mind.

"You look at me like you think I know,
I look at you like I'm ready to blow,
You make me so mad, you make me want to scream,
But you're my boss, and I'm not your queen,
I thought you were special,
Someone I'd want to get to know
I thought you were sexy,
I thought we could grow,
But you're just an asshole,
A king without a crown,
And I'm just your maid,
And I'm not about to go down."

I laughed at my last line. "So classy, Savannah," I mumbled to myself as I stepped out of the shower. "What did you think was going to happen, anyway? You don't even know him."

I grabbed a towel and headed back into the bedroom, then froze in my tracks. "What are you doing in here?"

Wade was sitting on the edge of my bed, his jacket off and the top buttons of his shirt undone.

"I came to apologize."

"Really, now?" I raised an eyebrow, not moving. "Go on, then."

"I'm sorry about tonight. I should have had you join us. It was rude of me." He leaned back in my bed. "I didn't mean to upset you or disrespect you."

"Well, you did."

"I know." He nodded. "You have to admit, this is a complicated situation."

"Oh?"

"We should have kept it completely professional." He jumped up off of the bed. "I shouldn't have kissed you."

"Well, you did."

"I shouldn't have had you sleeping in my bed last night."

"Again, you did."

"I shouldn't have touched you." He stopped in front of me.

"You know my response."

"I shouldn't have slipped my finger inside of you." He touched my bare shoulder.

"Wait, what?" I frowned. "You didn't do that."

"Not yet." He pressed his lips against mine and kissed me hard. As he did that his hand slipped under my towel and between my legs. His tongue found its way into my mouth, and I melted against him, loving the warm taste of whiskey on his lips. I felt his finger stroke me then gasped as he slid it inside. He growled against my lips as I pressed against him, my legs weak. The feel of his finger inside of me made me tremble. As much as I wanted to push him away, I couldn't. The taste of him was like a drug, and his finger was doing things to me that I didn't want to stop.

"Oops." His eyes twinkled as he pulled away from me.

"Don't *oops* me," I muttered as he continued fingering me.

"You know what else I shouldn't have done?" He pulled his finger out of me and pulled me into his arms, his finger running through my hair.

"What?" I gazed up at him, my heart racing. "Actually, don't answer that. If you think one half-assed apology is going to make me slip back into your bed, then you're out of your mind."

"I don't think that." He took my hand and began to gently back me up toward the bed. "I was moving too fast for you. I want to show you that I'm sorry."

"Okay. Well, I'm not going to say apology accepted, but rather pending."

"Pending?" He grinned as he took another step toward me and I took another step closer to the bed.

"Yeah." I sniffed. "I'm still deciding whether or not to accept it."

"Well, let me apologize to you in another way."

The back of my legs bumped the mattress, and I shivered, exquisitely conscious of the fact that I was in nothing but a towel. "What other way?"

"I never should have made you come with my tongue." He winked and pushed me onto the bed.

"Wade!" I gasped, my face blushing. "I'm not sure this is a good idea."

"You don't?" He ripped the towel off me, his pupils dilating as he took in my naked body. I lay there, surprised that I wasn't more self-conscious as he gazed down at me. He got onto the bed next to me. "Let me apologize to you in another way, Savannah. Don't you want me to?" He grazed my stomach with his fingers then moved his hand up to stroke my nipple, never taking his eyes off mine. "Can I kiss you?"

I nodded in response, not trusting myself to speak and as his lips met mine, filling me with a warm glow that I never wanted to end. His lips left mine and kissed down my body, his tongue tracing the valley between my breasts and then farther. He kissed down my stomach then pushed my thighs apart before lowering his mouth directly on my heat. I cried out as he took my clit into my mouth, sucking on it with such sweet intensity that desire bloomed in my very core. He licked me and teased me, and my fingers gripped the sheets as the tip of his tongue flicked against me.

"Ohhhh!" I cried out as his tongue slipped inside of me. I could barely control myself as his tongue fucked me, his hands gripping the side of my body. My body was made of fire, and I never wanted it extinguished. My thighs tightened around his face as his tongue slipped in and out of me, lightly teasing my clit as it moved back and forth. I could feel how wet I was against his lips, and I didn't even care. I just wanted to come. I needed to come. Everything was forgiven and forgotten. If he could make me feel like this, what did I care if he wanted me to cook for him?

Suddenly he moved up. "I need to see your face," he growled. "I need to see your face when you come." He lay down flat and pulled me onto him. "Sit on my face."

"What?" My eyes widened as his fingers played with my breasts.

"I want you to ride my face. I want you to grind your juicy pussy lips against me, I want to fuck you with my tongue, and I want to see your face as you come on me."

"Wade," I licked my lips nervously. "I don't know. I ..."

"Shh." He pulled me up and shifted me down and before I knew it, my pussy was directly above his face. He pushed my hips down and once again his lips found my core. I grabbed a hold of the headboard and moved back and forth on his face, crying out as his tongue flicked my clit and his beard teased my thighs. He pulled my hips down more and his tongue entered me, feeling even deeper than it had before. I cried out as I gyrated on his face and I could see him looking up at me, a dark intensity in his eyes. He ate me out as if his life depended on it. An orgasm began to swell deep within me. His tongue seemed to move deeper and deeper, tapping something inside of me.

I screamed. The pleasure was almost too much. I moved even faster on his face, and then my orgasm hit, powerful and hard. I rocked back and forth as he continued to lap me off. When the waves subsided, I rolled off of him and looked over at his grinning face, slick with my juices.

"You tasted better than that dinner did, that's for sure." He pulled me into his arms and kissed me. I could taste myself on him, but I didn't care. "You're so fucking hot, Savannah. I want to be inside of you so badly right now," he groaned.

I reached my hand down to his pants and ran my fingers along his hard erection. His hand grabbed mine and pulled it away. "If you continue doing that, tonight is going to go very differently."

"How's that?" I pressed my fingers harder against his cock.

"Savannah," his voice was a low growl, "I'm sorry about earlier. I'll try not to be as much of an ass as I was tonight."

"Oh, yeah?"

"Yeah." He then rolled off the bed and stood up. "I think my apology will be accepted now, yeah?" He looked down at me and licked his lips. "I hurt your feelings earlier, but now I've made you come. I think that more than makes up for you getting upset at having to do your job."

My jaw dropped at his words. He started chuckling, and I grew furious. This man really was playing with me, in more ways than one.

"Night, Savannah. I have to go and call Henry now. I'll see you at breakfast." And with that, he was out of the door.

I rolled over so that my face was pressed into the pillow and screamed into it. What had just happened? I was totally in over my head.

I grabbed my phone and text Lucy;

. . .

Savannah: You up?

    Lucy: Yup, why? How was your night?

    Savannah: Guess ...

Lucy: Well, seeing as you're texting me, I'm guessing you didn't give up your v-card.

Savannah: No, I didn't, though I did orgasm.

Lucy: OMG, what? Tell me more! Now.

Savannah: Wade went down on me.

Lucy: OMG! No way.

Savannah: Yeah! :P

Lucy: So you had fun?

Savannah: His tongue felt amazing. Sorry for TMI.

Lucy: Girl, it's me. There is no such thing as too much information. Tell me more. Did you return the favor?

Savannah: Nah. He went down on me to apologize.

Lucy: Uh oh, apologize for what?

Savannah: Well, let's just say I wasn't invited to the dinner. I was the help.

Lucy: Ooh ...

Savannah: Yeah, so he decided to apologize.

Lucy: I'm not sure what he's apologizing for?

Savannah: Treating me like the help.

Lucy: I hate to be rude, but aren't you?

Savannah: Ugh! :(

Lucy: I mean, I know you kinda like him, but you're his assistant, right? Not his girlfriend.

Savannah: Lucy! Sigh!

Lucy: Do you hate me?

Savannah: No, I guess you're right. I didn't look at it like that.

Lucy: Yeah, I think your feelings for him overwhelmed you.

Savannah: I guess so. He's just so hard to read. I almost feel like he's playing games with me.

Lucy: Are you having fun?

Savannah: Yes and no. I mean, he's hard to read, and it's not exactly the job of my dreams, but he pays well and if he keeps giving me orgasms, I'll be quite happy.

Lucy: I need to meet a man to give me orgasms. Lots and lots of orgasms.

Savannah: So you think I should forgive him?

Lucy: That doesn't sound like much of an apology to me. Seems like it was just an excuse to get into your panties.

Savannah: Ugh. You might be right. Ha ha.

Lucy: So … are you in his bed right now?

Savannah: No, I'm in my bed and he's in his.

Lucy: Ohhh, okay. I thought you wanted to figure out what he's working with?

Savannah: I do, but I think for tonight he can stew in his own mess and wish I was there.

Lucy: Ha ha, I bet he's wishing you were there right now.

Savannah: I hope so. I just can't figure it out.

Lucy: You will, girl. At some point you will. Men aren't like us. They don't hide their feelings. You'll figure out what he's about sooner or later.

Savannah: True. Thanks, girl. Sweet dreams!

Lucy: Sweet dreams! Night, girl.

CHAPTER 13

The next week passed as if nothing had ever happened between us. Wade didn't try to kiss me or get me into his bed again, and I avoided all physical contact with him.

We got into a consistent schedule. I woke up at 6:30 a.m., made his breakfast, and then went to shower. He usually had morning conference calls that he took by himself, though sometimes I was present to type up notes. After his calls, I would do whatever research he asked for and make lunch. We would usually eat lunch at the kitchen table or outside in the garden. After lunch, I would head to the library to follow up on emails, and he would head to his office to do whatever it was he did. Nothing was out of the ordinary. No other dinner parties were planned. Other than the fact that I lived in his home, it was just like a regular job and boss-assistant relationship.

"Good morning, Savannah." Wade walked in from the pool, a towel wrapped around his waist and his eyes on the coffee machine. "Coffee ready?"

"Yes, let me get you a cup."

"What's for breakfast this morning?"

"Scrambled eggs on toast with fried tomatoes."

"Sounds good." He nodded, grabbed his coffee and made his way back out of the kitchen. "Will you bring it to the office for me? I'm going to eat breakfast while I start working."

"Sure." I was disappointed that he was still acting so distant from me. Why was he being distant towards me? Shouldn't I be the one who was acting distant towards him? "Hey can I ask you a question?" I called after him.

He turned around to stare at me with a tilt of his head. "Sure, go ahead."

"Are you mad at me or something?" I put my hands on my hips. "You've just been different since the night of ... the dinner party."

"I have?" He looked surprised. "I didn't realize."

"You didn't realize?" I took a step closer to him. "Really? You have me sleeping in your bed, you kiss me, and then you stop, and you notice nothing different?"

"I didn't realize you enjoyed my kisses so much." His eyes peered into mine. "You never said."

"Wade, you went down on me." My face was now bright red.

"To apologize."

"An apology happens with words, not your tongue."

"Words happen with my tongue, too, though." He winked.

"You know what I mean." I sighed. "I just don't really know what's going on here."

"What do you mean?" He frowned. "I hired you as my assistant, I pay you as my assistant, you work as my assistant, nothing more and nothing less. I'm sorry if you were hoping for more."

"I didn't say I was hoping for more. I'm not even the one

that approached you." I was furious. "You're always twisting things to suit your narrative."

"Savannah, why don't you take the evening off? Maybe go to the village and participate in the open mic night tonight?" He shrugged. "Let off some steam, maybe you've been working too much."

"Maybe, whatever." I turned away from him and mumbled under my breath. "Frigging Dr. Jekyll and Mr. Hyde in the flesh."

"Sorry, what did you say, Savannah?"

"Nothing. I'll bring your breakfast through in a few minutes." I pursed my lips as I headed back to the stove. I was done with this asshole. So done.

"Don't forget to wear your uniform when you serve me," he added as he walked away.

I was almost positive he was trying to goad me, but I didn't let myself react. I had dealt with enough men to know that plenty of them were assholes, and it looked like Wade was one of them. I'd dated guys who really seemed to like me and then had completely ghosted me. There had been many nights I'd sat by the phone hoping for a return call or text that had never come. I had been on dates that had seemed to go well and ended in a kiss, only to have the guy snub me the next time he saw me. I considered these men to be boys. Immature, ignorant, and totally annoying boys. Lucy called them fuckboys. I was pretty sure she was using the term incorrectly, but I felt like it was appropriate. Wade Hart was definitely a fuckboy. What an asshole he was! How dare he go down on me and pleasure me and then act like nothing happened?

Not that I wanted anything to happen … but I still wanted the option.

"Yes, sir," I mumbled back and turned off the stove.

Once I was sure he was back in his office, I headed to my room to put my uniform on.

And then I had an idea. A sexy, naughty idea. He wanted me to wear my uniform, did he?

I pulled off my panties and bra and pulled on the skirt and top. I'd serve him and give him a show, and tease him, just for fun. And if he tried to make a move, I'd blank him and feign disinterest. I wouldn't let him know that I'd been having sexy dreams about him for the last week and that I was hornier than I'd ever been in my lie. I wouldn't let him know that I'd told Lucy that I'd wanted him to be the one to take my virginity.

Oh, no. There was no way he was getting near my hot spot ever again. I wouldn't let him kiss me on the lips or the pussy. He was done, as far as I was concerned. But that didn't mean I was above teasing him. I saw the way his eyes watched me when he thought I wasn't looking. Well, he was going to learn a lesson. You didn't play around with Savannah Carter. If you did, you got burned.

"Burned, burned, burned. You're going down, Wade Hart. You're going *down*." I grinned to myself as I grabbed a pair of heels I'd gotten in town and walked down the corridor and back to the kitchen. "I'll serve you breakfast in the office all right."

My heels click clacked as I walked down the corridor, and I could feel small whooshes of cool air between my legs with each stride. I grabbed a tray and a plate and two slices of whole grain bread. I didn't bother toasting them. Then I piled on the scrambled eggs and added a small dollop of hot sauce on the eggs the way Wade liked it. I poured some orange juice into a glass, grabbed a banana, some silverware, and a napkin, and made my way to Wade's office.

"You got this, Savannah. Do not chicken out," I whispered to myself as I walked. I stopped outside his door and knocked on his door.

"Yes?" he called out.

"It's me, your breakfast is ready."

"Okay, come in Savannah," he said, and then I heard him say, "One moment, please."

I walked into his office, sashaying my hips back and forth, but Wade didn't look up.

"Where would you like it, Mr. Hart?" I said in my sweetest voice, hoping to draw his attention.

"Any open space you see." Still he didn't look up. I pursed my lips and looked on his desktop for an empty space. I walked up to the desk and placed the tray down.

"Anything else, Mr. Hart?"

"No." His voice was curt. This asshole couldn't even acknowledge me as I served him.

"Are you sure, sir?"

"I'm sure." He typed something into his computer. I walked over to the side of his desk and tapped him on the shoulder. Finally, he looked up at me, his eyes narrow and distant. "Yes?"

"I was just wondering if you wanted any coffee?" I asked him and leaned over his desk to grab a pen. As I straightened back up, I brushed my breasts against his arm.

"No." He stilled as his eyes looked down at my chest. I knew that he could see my nipples through the flimsy material and smiled slightly. "Was there anything else, Savannah?"

"I was wondering if you could help me with something ..."

"With what?"

"I've got this itch, you see ..."

"What itch?" His lips twitched slightly.

"Well," I pushed his chair back and sat in his lap. "It's on my back."

"Savannah," he whispered in my ear. "I don't think you want to do this."

"Do what?" I moved back and forth on his lap, feeling my skirt riding up as I moved.

"Savannah, stop." His hands gripped my waist, but I still continued rubbing back and forth slightly. I grinned as I felt him growing hard beneath me.

"Can you scratch my back, please?" I whispered. He sighed and scratched my back for me. "A bit higher, a bit to the right, yes, right there," I moaned, moving back and forth on him and held onto the side of his thighs. "Yes, that's the spot. Oh, yes!" I cried out as I felt myself growing wet on his lap.

"Savannah?" He stopped scratching my back, and I felt his right hand slipping between my legs and moving up. His fingers brushed against my wet pussy. "You have no panties on?"

"Oops, did I forget to put them on?" I reached my fingers down and placed them over his hand moving them back and forth on my clit. I leaned my neck back and rested my head on his chest and closed my eyes. This hadn't been a part of the plan, but it felt *so* good. His fingers glided against me, and I gasped as he slipped one inside of me.

"Do you like this?" he whispered in my ear. "Is this what you wanted, Savannah? What you needed?"

"Yes." I couldn't even deny it. I needed him to keep touching me. "Don't stop."

"I think we'd better." He slid his fingers out. "I fear that I'm already in a bit of trouble."

"Trouble?" I opened my eyes and looked up into his face. "What are you talking about? Why are you in trouble?"

"I wasn't ignoring you, Savannah." He smirked as I sat up, his fingers still between my legs. "I was on a call."

"Okay, and?"

"A video conference call." He pointed to the laptop screen on the desk where the flashing green light above the screen alerted me to the fact that the camera was rolling.

"Oh, my God, why didn't you tell me?" I jumped up off of his lap and ran to the far side of the room. "How could you let me ..." My voice trailed off as I knew I couldn't really blame him. That had really been all me. Oh, my God, had a bunch of strange men just seen me giving Wade a lap dance and watched him fingering me. Please no!

I scurried to the door. Talk about a walk of shame!

"Savannah, wait!" Wade held up his hand and pressed a button on his laptop before looking up at me. "If you want to come back in forty-five minutes, we can finish what you started." He grinned. "Maybe this time with no one watching us."

"You wish." I shook my head and slammed the door behind me. I could hear him laughing and wondered if it was possible to die of embarrassment. What had I been thinking? Everything was going from bad to worse, and I was making myself look desperate.

I slipped my heels off and crept back to my room, where I quickly changed into a pair of jeans and a tank top. Who did I think I was fooling, going into his office without any underwear? I was playing with fire. What if he'd slipped his cock out and entered me while I'd been on his lap? What if he'd bent me over his desk and taken me? Did I really want my first time to be something so risqué?

I collapsed onto the bed as I realized that I didn't care. Wade Hart had gotten under my skin and I wasn't thinking properly. All I could think about was his touch. I wanted more from him, and I wanted him to want more from me. How could he have gone down on me and then just moved on? Why wasn't he chasing me?

I groaned into my pillow, frustrated. I didn't have much

experience with men, but I was pretty sure that I was falling right into his trap. I was about to head back to the kitchen when I decided to text Gordon back to see if he'd be at the pub later. I needed a change of scenery, and I needed a friend.

Savannah: Hey Gordon, will you be at the open mic tonight?

Gordon: Hey girl, I was wondering what happened to you. Yes, I'll be there. You?

Savannah: Yes, I need to get out of this house.

Gordon: Oh, no, it's going that badly?

Savannah: Let's just say that Wade isn't my favorite person.

Gordon: You're not going to quit, are you?

Savannah: No, not at all.

Gordon: I've always been curious to see Hart Manor. Is it glamorous?

Savannah: It's nice. Not too ostentatious.

Gordon: Aww, cool. So what time will you be there tonight?

Savannah: I'm thinking 7?

Gordon: Perfect. I'll see you there. Are you going to perform?

Savannah: You betcha. You?

Gordon: Yes!

Savannah: Excited to hear another one of your monologues.

Gordon: Thanks! I'm looking forward to hearing your poems. Stay strong, and I'll see you later.

Savannah: Bye.

. . .

I sat up on the bed and headed back towards the kitchen to clean up. As I walked past Wade's office, I could hear him talking, but I didn't stop to listen. I was about to call Lucy to update her on the morning's events when the doorbell rang. I waited to see if Wade was going to come out of his office, but when he didn't, I headed towards the front door. I knew it wasn't Henry because he would have just walked in and made himself at home.

A beautiful woman with dark sunglasses and a wide-brimmed hat stood on the doorstep.

"Hello, can I help you?"

"Where's Wade?" The woman pushed past me and sniffed as she entered as if she expected to smell something bad.

"He's in his office and he's busy. Can I help you?" My voice was a little cooler now. I hadn't appreciated the way she'd just walked into the house without being invited in, though I guess that meant she wasn't a vampire.

"I'm his mother, silly girl. Go and fetch him."

"He's on a video call." I looked her over more carefully now. So, this was his mother, the woman who had broken his father's heart.

She took off her sunglasses, looking me over with cold blue eyes. "And who are you?" She had a slight accent to her voice, an odd mix between French and English. I wondered if she was faking it and was just a bad actress.

"I'm Savannah Carter, Wade's assistant."

"Oh." She sniffed. "Is he not paying you well?"

"Excuse me?"

"You're not exactly dressed for success, are you?" She sniffed again. "I suppose you millennials really don't care about your appearance."

"I'm working in a home office. Wade hasn't complained about my attire."

"I suppose he's too nice." She yawned. "I'm bored, and I'm thirsty. Some coffee would be nice."

"Uhm, okay. This way, please." I closed the door behind her and headed to the kitchen. I was starting to understand why Wade wasn't a huge fan of his mom. She was a bitch. With a capital B.

"I *do* know which way the kitchen is. I used to live here." Her snooty voice echoed through the corridor. "In fact, I chose this house." She brushed past me and walked into the kitchen. "I have no idea why Wade has chosen to keep it." Her mouth dropped as she surveyed the mess in the kitchen. "Tell me, dear," She turned to me with narrowed eyes. "Are you really the assistant or are you another sort of paid help?"

"Sorry, what?" I went to the sink to fill the kettle. "I'm not sure what you mean."

I studied her while I ran the tap. Wade's mother was impeccably dressed. She reminded me of the actress Grace Kelly. She really was beautiful, but there was a coldness in her that made me want to shrivel up inside. I put the kettle on the burner and began to clear up the dishes from breakfast.

"Are you slow, dear?" She shook her head. "Let me spell this out for you." She wrinkled her nose as I scraped the remaining egg into the trash. "Are you Wade's assistant or his whore?"

"Excuse me?" My mouth dropped open as I turned to her. "What did you just say to me?"

"There's no need to be dramatic, girl. I was simply asking you a question." She looked me over again. "But you're definitely not Wade's type." She smirked. "I'll have my coffee by the pool." She looked me up and down and then headed outside.

I watched her go and sighed before hurrying to Wade's office. I knocked on the door and entered before he could say anything.

"Yes, Savannah." He grinned as I walked into his office. "Can you give me ten minutes? I'm not quite ready."

"Ready for what?"

"My lap dance."

I blushed. "That is not why I'm here. Also, I'm mad at you. How could you touch me while we were on camera?"

"Well, I think it was you who started it, don't you?" He laughed, his head going back. "But don't worry, the camera only shows my shoulder and above. My accountants didn't see anything other than an overly friendly maid sitting on my lap."

"I'm not your maid." I knew I sounded huffy, but after dealing with his mom, I wasn't in the mood for any crap.

"I know, you're my assistant." He smiled. "Who likes to go commando when she sits on my lap."

"Your mom is here." I cut him off.

The words wiped the cocky smirk right off his face. "What did you say?"

"Your mom is here."

"Fuck it." He stood up with a sigh. "Where exactly is she?"

"She went to sit by the pool while she waits for me to serve her a coffee." I rolled my eyes. "You know your job advertisement really was a lie."

"It was?"

"I spend more time in the kitchen than I do anywhere else."

"Would you rather spend more time in the bedroom?"

"Would you like to feel my fist in your face?"

He held up his hands. "I was just asking a question. I was wondering if you needed more sleep."

"No, you weren't. You were wondering if I would rather be your whore."

"My whore? Whoa! Where did that come from?" He

looked surprised as he gazed at my fuming face. "Are you okay, Savannah?"

"Do I look okay? Your mom flat-out asked I was your whore, and then when I emphatically told her no, she called me ugly. Well, she didn't exactly say I was ugly," I admitted, "but she implied it."

"You're not ugly, Savannah." Wade stepped forward and stroked my cheek. "Far from it."

"Just because I'm not all fancy like her," I grumbled. "Sorry for getting upset, but I thought you should know she's here."

"Yes, I guess I needed to know." He made a face. "Not that I really want to see her."

"She's your mom, though."

"In the biological sense, maybe. She doesn't actually feel like a mom, though. Let me go and see what she wants." He took my hand. "I guess the lap dance will have to wait until later."

"How about until never?"

"You're a hard one to read, Savannah Carter." There was a small smile on his face. "You come into my office to seduce me this morning, and now you're acting like you don't want me."

"I'm not the one that's hard to read, you're the..." I sighed. "I don't get you. And I didn't come to your office to seduce you."

"You sure about that?"

"I just came to tease you," I admitted. "That's all."

"You came to tease me with no panties and no bra?" He raised an eyebrow. "I'd hate to see what you'd do if the plan *was* to seduce me."

"Well, you will never know." I glared at him, feeling hot and bothered. He was correct, of course—what the hell had I been thinking by not wearing panties? Was I hoping it would just slip in?

Ugh, my thoughts were getting dirty, and I didn't want to think about any part of Wade slipping into me.

"I wouldn't bet on that, if I was you." He winked and then made a face. "I'll head out to see what my mom wants. Will you bring the coffee out in about fifteen minutes?"

"Sure." Without thinking, I touched his arm. "Good luck." I smiled at him, and his expression changed slightly. He looked like he was surprised by my gesture, and I looked away. "I hope it goes well."

"Thank you, Savannah. I appreciate it." He took my hand and squeezed it. "Sometimes I think you could make me a believer." For just a moment, his expression flickered, making him look more like a vulnerable man, not the cocky bastard I knew he was.

"Believer in what?" I asked.

"The unbelievable." He smiled wryly. "Let me go and deal with the Wicked Witch of the West." He lightly kissed my cheek and headed outside.

I stood there, touching the side of my face where I could still feel his lips and staring at the French doors he'd just walked through. Wade was a complicated man. He was dealing with issues I didn't even pretend to understand. If his mom had abandoned him and his brother and father when he was young, he most probably suffered from trauma. From the way he acted, it seemed to be that his mother still affected him. And maybe that explained why he didn't seem to believe in love. A lone tear rolled down my face as I thought about the hopeful yet resigned look in his face as he'd just said *the unbelievable*. Did I have it in me to make him believe? Did I even believe?

My heart hurt for him and hurt for me, for reasons I

didn't fully understand. What exactly was happening between us? What did I want? I truly didn't know, and it scared me.

Something had shifted between us. It was obvious that we were both attracted to each other, but somehow it felt like there was more going on. Was that just wishful thinking on my part?

As I walked back to the kitchen and made the coffee, I wondered if reading and understanding men would ever get easier, or if I was destined to a life of uncertainty and cluelessness.

CHAPTER 14

"Why if it isn't my favorite Georgia girl." A sweet voice greeted me as soon as I entered the pub. I looked to the side and saw Beryl from the cafe.

"Hi." I gave her a little wave, not bothering to correct her. "Nice to see you."

"How are you getting on up there at Hart manor?" She looked at me knowingly. "Got you all sorts of twisted up inside?"

"It's going fine, thanks."

"There are so many secrets between those Hart brothers." Beryl's voice lowered. "You seen anything strange up there?"

"Nope." I shook my head, wondering what I could say to distance myself away from her.

"I'm not one to gossip, you know, but funny things have gone on there." She pursed her lips. "Things that aren't right."

"Oh?" I studied her face for a few seconds. "What sort of things?" If she was going to keep dropping hints, she might as well expand on them.

"Well, let's just say that all the Hart Brothers aren't good in the head." She raised an eyebrow. "There's a reason he lives in Herne Hill Village, you know. He didn't just come here for fun."

"Wade?" It had to be Wade she was talking about. Henry had said he didn't live in the village and was only visiting. Though, now that I thought about it, that struck me as odd. If he was visiting, why didn't he stay with his brother? He had implied it was because Wade had women over, but except for Etta, who'd left after dinner, I hadn't seen Wade with any other women.

"Wade Hart is the oldest brother." Beryl sounded like she was talking to herself. "I would consider him the best-looking brother."

"Uhm, okay." This was going nowhere fast.

"You just watch yourself, dear. There are men in this world that will bed a pretty girl like you just to get their own way. It doesn't mean they like you, it just means that you can help them."

"Uhm, I'll remember that, thank you."

"Savannah, there you are." Gordon came running over to me with a huge smile on his face and he gave me a big hug. "I was wondering if you were here yet."

"I just made it."

"Great, let me buy you a drink, and you'll have to tell me all about what's going on at Hart Manor."

"Sounds like a plan. I think I'd like a cocktail tonight." I smiled at him and then nodded towards Beryl. "Gordon, do you know Beryl? She runs the cafe in town."

"Nice to meet you, Beryl. I think I've been in your cafe a few times."

"Mhmm, yes, I've seen you." She nodded, her eyes looking at me with a knowing look. "You have a good evening, Savannah. Don't forget what I told you."

I began to follow Gordon to the bar, but I got only a step

before Beryl grabbed me and pulled me back. "If something comes too easy, that's because it is," she whispered. "Those Hart boys are no good. Not a one of them. No matter how much they smile at you or how many drinks they buy you."

"Well, Wade isn't here tonight, so I don't think he'll be buying me any drinks tonight. Thanks though, Beryl." I pulled away from her and hurried to the bar to join Gordon. "Sorry about that." I rolled my eyes. "Beryl was just warning me about Wade."

"Oh, yeah? Does she think the big bad wolf wants you for dinner?" He laughed. "Want a lemon drop? That's their drink of the night, and they're serving two-for-one right now."

"You definitely can't beat two for one, yes, please." I nodded enthusiastically. "I will most probably down the first drink in ten seconds, so it's a good idea to have the second one ready to go."

"A woman after my own heart." He winked at me.

As I looked into his flirtatious face, I realized that I needed to make sure we were both on the same page. I'd hate to think that I'd gotten it wrong and Gordon was straight and making a move on me.

"I don't think anyone has said those words to me before." I laughed and then because I was feeling brave, I asked, "Do you have a girlfriend?"

"A girlfriend?" He raised an eyebrow and burst out laughing. "Oh, no, I don't do girlfriends." And then he paused. "I know you're not asking for yourself, though."

"Oh, how do you know?"

"You're so obviously smitten with Wade."

"No, I'm not." I shook my head vehemently, my hair swinging around my face. "Trust me, I'm not."

"Methinks thou doth protest too much." He grinned.

"I love Hamlet." I changed the subject. "Shakespeare really was one of the greats, wasn't he?"

"He was." He handed me a glass. "Here's your first drink. Have a sip, and then let's go and sit down. I can't wait to hear all about your week."

"Are you sure?" I was surprised at his interest. Not many people wanted to listen to some random person they'd recently met complain so much.

"I love a good gossip." He nodded as he paid for the drinks and then we looked around for a seat. "Over here." He moved past me and made his way to two seats close to the front of the stage. "Actually …" he paused and moved back. "We can't laugh and talk if we sit at the front, let's go to the back."

"Sounds like a plan to me." We took our seats, and I took a long gulp of my drink. It tasted sweet and strong, just as I liked it. "This is so good, thanks, Gordon."

"Don't thank me, next round is on you." He laughed and drank from his beer. "So, how have you been? What's been going on with you?"

"Oh, just the same old, same new, working for my boss, hooking up with my boss, meeting my boss's bitchy mom and hating her."

"Wait, wait, wait." His eyes widened. "You hooked up with Wade? And his mom is in town?"

"When I say hooked up, I mean made out, not sex— well, not full sex." I blushed. "Just oral."

"You went down on Wade?"

"No." I grinned.

Gordon threw his head back and laughed. "You go, girl." He held his hand up and high-fived me. "You get yours."

"I'm glad you're not upset."

"Upset?" He looked confused for a moment then

laughed. "Oh, you mean jealous? I bat for the other team, if that wasn't apparent."

"I mean, I never like to assume." I blushed. "Sorry."

He just kept on grinning. "Girl, you have nothing to apologize for." He shook his head. "Plus, like I said, I could tell you were into Wade. And even if I was straight, you're too nice of a girl for me. I need new friends, not a fuckbuddy."

"I'm glad we can be friends."

"Me, too. I really want to see that mansion you work in." He laughed, but a shiver of uneasiness crept up the back of my neck. This was the second time he'd mentioned seeing Wade's home. Why did he care so much?

I shook my head. "I can't really have visitors over, but maybe in a few weeks, Wade will loosen up and let me have people over."

"Yeah, what is he, your prison warden?" Gordon chugged his beer. "Why can you not have friends over now?"

"I wish I knew," I answered with a shrug.

We both quieted down as the lights dimmed and the host welcomed everyone to the open-mic night. I sat back and sipped on my drink, feeling warm and sightly buzzed. I was glad to be out of the house, away from Wade and his mom. I wondered how long his she was going to stay. With any luck, she would be gone by the time I got home and that wouldn't see her in the morning. She really didn't seem like a nice person, and I was starting to understand why Wade resented her so much.

The sounds of the clock chiming greeted me as I stumbled through the front door giggling and hiccupping. It was 3 a.m., and I was drunk. I'd gotten a car ride home and left the Range Rover in town. I'd have to ask Wade to take me into town in the morning to pick it up. Hopefully, he wouldn't be upset.

"Of course he'll be upset," I giggled to myself as I made my way through the hallway, banging into the wall as I walked.

"Savannah, is that you?" Wade's voice sounded from the living room and I froze. Shit!

"Nope." Hiccup.

"Savannah?"

I put a finger to my lips. "I'm a figment of your imagination." Hiccup. Giggle.

"Savannah?" Wade was now standing in front of me, looking larger than life. He was wearing white briefs and a navy-blue t-shirt. The briefs left nothing to the imagination, and I swallowed hard.

"Is that a banana or are you just happy to see me?" I reached out. "Ooh, hard."

"That's the handle of an umbrella, Savannah." He looked down into my face. "Are you drunk?"

"No." Hiccup. I leaned back into the wall. "Is bitchy still here?"

"Who?" He frowned.

"Your mom."

"Oh." He laughed. "Yes, she's in one of the guest rooms."

I groaned. "That sucks."

"Indeed it does." He swept me up into his arms.

"What are you doing?" I gaped up at him.

"I'm carrying you to bed." He strode down the corridor. "You seem to be having trouble walking."

"No, I don't. I'm walking just fine." Hiccup.

"I hope you didn't drive home."

"No, I left the car in town. We have to get it tomorrow."

"We do, do we?" He sounded amused. "So, who were you drinking with?"

"My friend."

"Your friend?" He frowned. "Not that man?"

"What man?"

"The man that texted you? Gecko?"

"Gecko?" I giggled uncontrollably for what felt like minutes. "You mean Gordon."

"Yes, I mean Gordon." He stopped outside his bedroom door, opened it and walked in.

"What are you doing? This isn't my room."

"I know." He carried me over to his bed, placed me on the mattress, and looked down at me. "Stay here, I'm going to get you some water and some crackers to eat. Do not move."

"You're the boss." I sank my head into the plush pillow and closed my eyes. "Whatever you want."

"That's the right answer." He chuckled, and I heard him leaving the bedroom. A few minutes later, he walked back and sat down on the next to me. "Drink this." He handed me a glass. I took the water from him gratefully and gulped it down. Then he handed me some saltines for me to nibble on. "How much did you drink?"

"Not that much, really." I sat up and leaned back against his headboard.

"And how much is not much?"

"Four lemon drops, one beer, and two shots of tequila."

"Ugh. You're going to be in for a bad morning tomorrow."

"I'll be fine." I looked at the clock on his desk and

groaned. "Though maybe not super great. I'm not sure if I'll be able to wake up to make your breakfast in time."

"Don't worry about my breakfast tomorrow."

"But what about your mom? Won't she be expecting me to cook for her?"

"You're not the cook of the house, Savannah. She can fend for herself." He ran his fingers through my hair. "It's a pity you're drunk because I want to kiss you very badly right now."

"So, why don't you?" I leaned forward, but he just shook his head.

"You need to have a shower first."

"I don't want to." I shook my head obstinately. "I just want to sleep."

"Have a quick shower." He pulled me off of the bed. "It will make you feel better and help to prevent a hangover in the morning."

"Will it really?"

"That's what I've been told."

"Fine." I headed for the door, but he grabbed my hand.

"Where do you think you're going?"

"To my room to have a shower."

"You're sleeping here tonight."

"But I still need to shower and put on my pjs." I didn't even protest at the thought of sleeping with him. It was just one night, and it would feel nice to sleep in his arms.

"You'll shower here, and I'll give you a t-shirt to wear."

"Fine." I was too tired to argue with him. I yawned and leaned my head against his chest. "You feel so warm and delicious." I looked up at his face. "And sexy." I reached up and touched his lips. "You have such juicy lips, I could just eat them."

"Well, hopefully not." He laughed. "Come on, Savannah, let's get you to the shower."

"Okay." I nodded, and then I frowned. "How come you're still awake?"

"I've been waiting on you to get home," he said gently. "You didn't say you'd be gone all night."

"I didn't know I had to say."

"So, were you on a date?" His voice sounded gruffer as he helped me get out of my clothes. "Did you kiss him goodnight?"

"Kiss who goodnight?"

'Gecko."

"Gecko? You mean Geico?" I started laughing again. Wade just frowned in response. "Oh, you mean Gordon." I grinned. "Gordon isn't interested in kissing me."

"Oh?" His eyes narrowed. "How do you know?"

"Ooh, I'm naked!" I gasped as the cool air hit my bare skin. I shook my finger in his face and giggled. "Don't go trying to have your wicked way with me, Wade."

"You wish, Savannah." He shook his head as he turned on the shower. "Now get into the shower."

"Are you going to get in with me?" I batted my eyelashes at him and gave him what I hoped was a sexy smile.

"I don't think that's a great idea." He shook his head with a wry smile. "In." He pointed at the shower.

I pouted. "I don't want to go in alone."

"Fine." He shook his head, muttered something under his breath, and grabbed my hand. "Come on." He led me into the shower and the lukewarm water poured over my skin.

"This is cold." I gasped as I pushed myself into him. "Why do you have your clothes on in the shower?"

"Because it's a good idea." He grinned.

"Nope." I grabbed the bottom of his t-shirt and pulled it up. He hesitated a moment and then lifted his arms up so that I could pull it all of the way off him. My fingers then ran down his chest, playing with his nipples and feeling his abs as the water drenched both of us.

"Savannah," he groaned as my fingers went south to pull his briefs off, "I think that's enough."

"Boo." I pouted.

Before I could say anything else, his lips crashed down on mine. I wrapped my arms around his neck and kissed him back, pushing my breasts against his chest and melting into him. His hands wrapped around my waist as he pushed me back against the wall, his lips falling to my neck. He then grabbed a bar of soap, wet it, and began to rub it over my body, gently down my arms and then to my shoulders and breasts. Tantalizingly, he made his way down to my stomach and then finally in between my legs.

He rubbed the soap onto his fingers and dropped the bar on the ground. He slipped his fingers in between my legs and rubbed back and forth, soaping up my clit and folds until my knees felt like they might buckle.

"You're not meant to put soap there like that," I mumbled as his fingers started rubbing my clit in circles. "It can lead to yeast infections."

He pulled his hand away, and I immediately grabbed it and put it back between my legs. "I didn't mean you should stop!"

He chuckled, but the sound cut off when I reached down and slipped my hand into his briefs. His cock was rock hard.

"Savannah …" he groaned. "I don't think …"

Before he could stop me, I pulled his briefs down. He stepped out of them, and I stared at his cock in awe. It was beautiful, and I wasn't even really into the look of them. But Wade's hardness thrust out, hard and thick and wet, and I couldn't wait to touch it.

"My turn," I said with a sweet smile.

"Here," he said, handing me the soap.

"Oh, not for that." I dropped to my knees, the water streaming down my face as I took him in my mouth.

He groaned as my lips met his skin. I had to open my mouth wide to suck him, and even then, I couldn't fit all of him inside. I bobbed up and down on his cock, licking it and sucking it with pleasure. He pulled on my hair and grunted as I blew him. I loved that I could feel him getting harder and harder as I took him in further and further, then reached up to play with his balls. His whole body suddenly stiffened and he pulled away from me. He grabbed his cock and stroked himself twice before he exploded into the shower, some of his warm cum hitting my face before being washed away by the water. He pulled me up to kiss me, and I kissed him back passionately.

"You didn't have to pull me away." I wrapped my hands around his hard butt.

"I did." His fingers played with my nipples as once again he pushed me up against the shower wall. "The first time I come inside of you, I want it to be in your pussy, not your mouth."

My legs trembled at his words. He started kissing my neck again, and I melted against him. He lifted me up, and I wrapped my legs around his waist. He groaned as he adjusted himself next to me. I felt his cock rubbing against my entrance, and I closed my eyes and moaned at how good it felt.

"I want to fuck you so badly," he whispered in my ear as he slipped a finger inside of me. "I wanted to go slow the first time, but I can't go slow right now. I just need to feel you." I kissed him hard, and he moved his mouth down to suck on my nipples. "I'm getting hard again already," he grunted as he rubbed the tip of his cock on my clit. The pleasure almost made me cry out. "Have you ever been fucked in the shower before, Savannah?" he asked as he rubbed against my entrance.

I suddenly realized what was happening, and I froze.

"Hey, what's wrong?" he asked.

"We can't—I can't do this." I pushed him back.

"What?" He blinked.

"You're not wearing a rubber."

"I'm clean."

"But pregnancy!"

"Aren't you on the pill?" He looked surprised. "I assumed you would have been on birth control if you had a boyfriend."

"I didn't have a boyfriend." I bit my lower lip. "That was a lie."

"So you're not on the pill at all?" He let me down. "You didn't *just* break up, did you?" He groaned. "Oh, Savannah." He looked at me naked body and sighed. "Come on, let's dry you off and we can go to the bed. I have condoms in my drawer."

"I don't know …" I leaned against the shower wall. I wanted him very badly. I wanted him to be my first, but not like this. Not when I was half-drunk. Not when I didn't really know where we stood. "You haven't even taken me out on a date," I blurted out.

He looked at me in surprise. "Sorry what?" He blinked as he turned the water off.

"You've never even taken me on a date, but you want to sleep with me."

"Are you joking?" We stepped out of the shower. "You weren't complaining about that when my tongue was inside of you, making you come. Or when my fingers …" He stopped and sighed as he held out a towel for me to step into. "But fine." He wrapped the towel around me and kissed my forehead. "How are you feeling?"

"Okay." I looked at his face to see if he was mad at me. "The shower took away some of my buzz."

"Good." He smiled. "Now, let's get you to bed."

"Do you want me to go to my own room now that you know there will be no sex for you tonight?"

He frowned. "I didn't invite you to my room for sex, Savannah. Come with me." He led me to his bedroom, and I watched as he opened a drawer and pulled out a long black t-shirt. "Put this on and get under the sheets."

"Okay," I grabbed the t-shirt and let the towel drop. He groaned at the sight of my naked body and then walked back into the bathroom.

"What are you doing to me?" he muttered.

I put his shirt on and got into the bed. I couldn't believe that I'd just told Wade Hart I wouldn't sleep with him when every fiber in my body wanted to sleep with him so badly. I lay there for what felt like ages, my eyelids getting heavier and heavier. It was only when Wade got into the bed that I realized I'd dozed off slightly.

He flicked the light off and settled into his side. I waited for him to wrap his arms around me but he did nothing. I shifted in the bed so that I was facing him. He was lying on his back, staring at the ceiling.

"What are you thinking about?" I asked him softly, and he looked over at me in surprise.

"I thought you were asleep."

"Nope. Why would you think that?"

"You were snoring." He laughed, and I rolled my eyes. "Sweet dreams, Savannah."

"That's it?" I moved closer to him and I saw his nostrils flaring as I moved my head to his shoulder and reached out and touched his chest.

"What do you mean, that's it?" He frowned as I stretched a leg over him. "What are you doing?"

"Getting comfortable."

"Savannah …" he groaned.

I slid my leg down his stomach, and my thigh grazed his bare cock. "You don't have anything on?" I grinned in the dark, tracing my fingers down his chest towards his cock.

"Savannah, stop." He grabbed my hand and pulled it up. ""I think it would be better for you to sleep on your side of the bed. Go to sleep."

"I don't want to go to sleep." I kissed his chest.

He pushed me onto my back and rolled on top of me. "So you want me to fuck you, then?" he growled. He grabbed my legs and pulled them over his shoulders and then leaned down to kiss me. "Do you want to feel my hard cock thrusting into you, you tease?" His fingers played with my nipples, and I could feel the tip of him rubbing my clit. Heat pooled between my legs.

"Wade," I moaned, desire and desperation growing in me.

"Oh, Savannah, what are you doing to me?" he groaned.

Abruptly, he moved down and buried his face in my pussy, his tongue entering me in one quick movement. His fingers rubbed me at the same time he was fucking me with his tongue. I grabbed his hair, shouting and shuddering as I quickly climaxed at his touch. He kissed back up my body and pulled me into his arms.

"Is that better?" he whispered in my ear as I snuggled against him, satiated and happy.

"Yes," I whispered as I closed my eyes. I could feel his hard cock against me and snuggled my ass against it. "Night, Wade."

"Night, Savannah," he snorted. "Once again, you're leaving me horny and blue."

I smiled at the agony in his voice as I drifted off to sleep.

CHAPTER 15

It felt like a hammer was pounding into my head when I woke up. I groaned and held my forehead in my hands.

"Good morning," Wade's deep voice greeted me.

I opened my eyes slowly and looked around the room as the events of the previous evening came flooding back. Oh, shit, I'd given him a blowjob in the shower and I'd nearly had sex with him …

And oh, shit, I'd complained because he hadn't taken me on a date.

I wanted to curl up into a ball and die, I was so embarrassed.

"Hungry?" Wade picked up a plate from a tray on the dresser and placed it on the sheet in front of me. "I made you some scrambled eggs and toast."

"Oh, you didn't have to do that." I blushed as I sat up. I looked over to the clock to see that it was 11 a.m. "Oh, no! It's so late. I'm so sorry."

"Don't be sorry." He smiled. "You only missed my breakfast, a conference call, and another meeting."

"Oh, no." I bit down on my lower lip, and he started laughing.

"It's okay, Savannah. I'm sure you're not going to make it a habit, getting drunk every night."

"No, no, of course not."

"Did you sleep well?"

"I did, thanks. You?"

"You want the truth?" He sat on the mattress and watched me eating my eggs and toast.

"The truth."

"I had blue balls like no one's business." He laughed. "I woke up at 5 a.m. and swam for over an hour."

"Oh, no!"

"Oh, yes." He nodded. "And then I had a cold shower and jerked off to images in my head of you blowing me last night." He grinned. "And I've been working ever since, so there you have it."

"Uhm, thanks for your honesty, I guess?" I winced. "You must think I'm a horrible assistant."

"Not horrible." He shook his head. "But definitely not the best."

"Wade!" I poked him in the shoulder.

"What?" He laughed. "You haven't even worked here a month and you've already gotten so drunk you missed a day of work."

"You and your mother drove me to drink," I grumbled. "Speaking of which, where is she?"

"She's gone to the village to do some shopping." He made a face. "I figured we could go out this afternoon, so you don't have to deal with her then, either."

"Go out?"

"Yes." He grinned. "I can show you a bit of the area."

"That would be cool." I took another bite of the buttery

toast and chewed. "Do you have time today? Or should you really be working?"

"I'm the boss, I always have time for a break."

"I guess that's true."

"And you're my assistant, so you do as I say."

"I do, do I?"

"Well, you should." He raised an eyebrow. "That's what you're paid for."

"I suppose so." I shrugged and then ate some eggs. "What time will we leave?"

"I'd love to leave in thirty minutes, if you can be ready by then?"

"Sure. Anything in particular I should wear?"

"No." He grinned. "Whatever you see fit."

"Really?"

"No, bring a swimsuit if you brought one."

"I didn't bring one," I lied.

He smirked. "I don't mind. I'm not opposed to skinny dipping." He shrugged. "Though I did tell you to bring one."

"You're not the boss of—" I stopped. He was very much still the boss of me.

He chuckled. "I wondered if you'd catch yourself. I'll go and make some sandwiches and then you can get ready.

"You really don't have to do that." I shook my head. "I should be making our lunch."

"But I invited you on this date, so I think it's okay."

"This is a date?" I couldn't keep the surprise out of my voice.

"Well, you seemed reluctant to sleep with me without us going on a date."

"So all this is so you can sleep with me?"

"I very much want to sleep with you, Savannah." He looked over my messy hair and still sleepy face. "You're nothing like I thought you would be like, you know that, right?"

"You're nothing like I thought you would be, either. Or rather, I'm not the person I thought I would be around someone like you."

"Someone like me?" He raised a single eyebrow and my heart melted a little more. Why did this handsome man want me so much? Was it because he hadn't had me yet? Or was it possible he actually liked me?

"You know what I mean."

'I don't, but I dare say that I will figure it out eventually."

"How was the open mic night last night?" He cocked his head to the side. "Will you tell me one of your poems today?"

"I don't know." I suddenly felt shy. "I don't want you to judge me."

"Judge you?" He shook his head. "I wouldn't do that."

"Really?"

"No comment." He winked and then walked towards his bedroom door. "Finish your breakfast and get ready."

After he left, I leaned back against the headboard and looked around the room. On my right was a large painting of a stag. I was surprised I'd never noticed it before. Possibly, I'd been too focused on Wade the previous times I'd been in the room to notice much else. The stag appeared to be standing in front of mountains and I stared at its antlers in awe. Such a striking painting.

"That's an original Edwin Landseer." A sharp voice carried through the room and my eyes flew to the door. There stood Wade's mother, her blond hair flowing around her face. Her eyes looked softer this morning and she walked into the bedroom. "'The Monarch of the Glen.'"

"Sorry, what?" I pulled the sheets a little closer around me.

"The name of the painting is 'The Monarch of The Glen.' Edwin Landseer painted it in 1851. My late husband purchased it for me when we were in London one summer." She walked up to it. "It's a beautiful painting, but not one I would have wanted in my bedroom." She looked back at me. "His use of light is quite magnificent, though, don't you think?"

"Yes." I nodded, surprised she was being so friendly to me. Well, that wasn't exactly the right word. She wasn't being friendly. She just wasn't being a bitch.

She turned away from the painting and looked thoughtfully at me. "You're not what I expected." She pursed her lips. "Though Wade has never been predictable. How long have you been fucking my son?"

"We're not sleeping together … well, not having sex." I mumbled. "It's not what you think."

"I'm sure it's exactly what I think." She shook her head. "My son has no heart, you know."

"That's not true."

"It is, but you most probably don't know him well enough yet." She sighed. "Wade lost his heart many years ago."

"Why do you say that?" I frowned and sat up. The sheet rolled down and exposed my black t-shirt.

"Well, you're not naked." She looked thoughtful. "Interesting."

"Uhm, I'm going to my room to shower now." I pushed the sheet further back and got out of the bed. "Have a nice morning."

"You don't like me, do you?"

I paused. Was she surprised I didn't like her? Did she suffer from the same split personality that Wade suffered from?

"I don't really know you." I wanted to leave, but I stood

there, unsure what the etiquette was in a situation like this. "I'm just Wade's assistant." I looked back at the bed and blushed. "This is just a new situation for me."

"You're young, aren't you?"

"I'm twenty-two, not that young."

"My son is thirty."

"He acts as if he's eighteen."

"Yes, he does, doesn't he?" She smiled suddenly. "He hates me with the immature petulance of a little boy."

"He doesn't hate you," I replied, but I couldn't meet her eyes. Suddenly I felt bad for this woman, even though I didn't really like her myself.

"You don't need to lie to me. I know my son. He blames me for his father's death."

"Maybe more for his heartache," I suggested.

"I didn't break Joseph's heart," she scoffed. "No matter what he told those boys."

"But you left them!" I accused her. "To go and be a model and hobnob with the rich and famous."

"So my son has shared his history with you." She walked over to me and stared in my eyes. "I can see from your face that you're passionate. You care about him, don't you?" She didn't wait for an answer. "You're in love with him." She tilted her head to one side, studying me. "You're not a gold-digger, are you?"

"Of course not!" I was indignant at the suggestion. "How dare you?"

"I dare many things, my child." She smiled. "You've got a mouth on you, don't you?" She tilted her head. "I guess I'm glad for that. It's very important to speak up for oneself."

"You don't seem to have any problems on that score."

"You think I'm a bitch, don't you? I wasn't always like this, you know. I used to be a happy girl. A fun one. A really nice girl." She shook her head. "Well, that's a lie. I've always been a bit vain. Maybe not so much nice as I was pure. A true believer in love."

"Well, you had Joseph in love with you, and he wrote you love letters and sent you presents and all sorts of things."

"How do you know about that?" Her eyes narrowed. "Surely Wade didn't tell you all that?"

"No." I pressed my lips together. "I found some old letters and photos in the library."

"I see." She nodded. "Joe was always a sentimental man. A narcissist and philanderer, but a sentimental one. He was one of those men who's more in love with the idea of love than anything else. He never loved anyone more than himself, you know." She shook her head. "But the past is the past."

"He loved you. And he loved his sons." For some reason, I felt the need to speak up for Joseph Hart, even though I never knew him. "And you left him and broke his heart. I think you're the only one that only cared about herself."

"You judge me quite harshly for someone that doesn't know me."

"I'm only going by what your son told me. Or does he not know you very well, either?"

"It's easy to judge, you know. When one doesn't know the truth." She turned away from me. "You should go and get ready for whatever it is you have to do today. I see that you have feelings for Wade, which pleases me. You might not be a gold-digger, dear, but I do have to warn you ..."

"Warn me about what?"

"Wade will still break your heart." She walked to the door then looked back at me over her shoulder, her eyes pitying. "My son is a good man, a handsome man, a strong man, but he lacks the ability to love." She looked me over. "You'd do well to remember that, *ma chérie*."

And then she walked out of the room, leaving me cold

and empty. Our talk affected me far more than her nasty words of the previous day. Yesterday, I'd been able to write her off as just being a bitch. Today, her words had pierced my soul.

I felt like crying and hurried to my room, wanting desperately to call Lucy. As soon as I'd shut the door, though, I realized my bag was still in Wade's room, so I went back out to get it. I retrieved it quickly and was on my way back to my room when I heard voices coming from the kitchen.

"What are you doing here, Mom?"

"I wanted to spend some time with my sons."

"You don't call first?"

"You didn't answer my calls, Wade."

"Then maybe you should have gotten the hint."

"Why are you so cruel to your mother?"

"Mom, you left Henry and me when we were kids. You don't get to play the emotional manipulation card."

"Your heart is so cold." She sighed. "If I'd known Joseph would have ..." Her voice trailed off. "Maybe Henry can come over for dinner, and the three of us can have a meal. That maid of yours, Savage, can serve us."

"Her name is Savannah, and she's not my maid. She won't be serving anything."

I stifled a burst of laughter. Funny how he wasn't saying that the week earlier when I was serving him, his brother, and that skank.

"Don't fuck her, Wade. Let the poor girl do her job without falling for you."

"She's not falling for me, Mother. And we're two grown adults. We can do what we want."

"She's barely twenty-two. Did she just graduate college?" his mother continued. "You can tell by looking at her that she doesn't have a clue. She doesn't know how to do her makeup or her hair and her clothes. Where did she buy them? Target?"

"Mom, that's enough."

"You can do so much better than her. My friend, Silviana, her daughter is visiting New York next week. I'd love to introduce you. She's just back from Milan. She's a model, you know."

"Mom, I don't need your help getting laid." He sounded frustrated. "Never have and never will."

"Obviously, you need some help or you wouldn't be sleeping around with the servants."

"She's my assistant."

"She's falling for you, you know." She sounded almost bored. "I can tell you feel for the girl but, Wade, you and I both know you would never marry her. She's not from our world. She's a nobody. And frankly, she must have been pretty desperate to take a job up here."

"Savannah and I are on the same page. She's working here for six months, and we're having some fun. Nothing more and nothing less." His tone was dismissive. "If I sleep with her, that's up to me."

"Just don't go getting the girl pregnant." His mom's voice was sharp. "There are enough bastard Hart children out there."

By this time, my heart was thudding in my chest so loudly I was surprised they hadn't heard it. I scurried back to my room before I got so angry that I started shouting at the both of them. Neither one of them talked about me with any real concern or respect, and that hurt me.

Well, Louisa's comments didn't hurt me because I'd already known she was a bitch and didn't care about anyone else, but Wade's comments had. The fact that he'd so casually dismissed any sort of real relationship between us had stung. And what about his mother's last comment? What bastard

Hart children were out there? Did Wade have a son? Or Henry? I couldn't really see either of them as fathers, but maybe that was what Louisa had been saying. Something was missing from their hearts. Maybe their parents' relationship had broken them in some irreparable way. Maybe Wade just wasn't capable of loving someone.

I turned on the shower and jumped in. The water poured over my skin and I couldn't help thinking that it was just a few hours ago that Wade had washed me so delicately with the soap. His mother was right, of course. I was falling for him. Hook, line and sinker. Body, mind and soul.

Maybe it was time to leave Herne Hill Village before I was too far gone.

CHAPTER 16

"Do you have your bikini with you?" Wade glanced at my small bag as we walked to his truck.

"I have it on." I pulled my tank top away from my chest. "Is that okay?"

"That's fine." He opened the side door of the truck open for me. "You going to get in."

"We're going in this?" I looked dubiously at the rusted-out sky-blue truck. "Does it run?"

"It's perfect for our needs. This beauty is a classic."

"It is?"

"It needs some exterior work, but she runs well. She's a '67 Chevy C10. She was born to run."

"A long time ago."

I cast another doubtful glance at the truck but slid inside and sat on the soft black leather seat. Wade shut the door behind me and walked around to the driver's side. I leaned over and opened the door for him and he smiled as he got in.

"Thanks." He looked surprised. "I wasn't expecting you to open the door for me."

"I'm a Florida girl. I have manners."

His eyes crinkled as he laughed. "I'm not sure that's what Florida girls are known for."

"Oh, what are they known for?"

"Alligator wrestling, lying on the beach, and shopping at the mall."

"Wow, you just described every girl in my high school class."

"You included? You wrestled the gators as well?"

"I was State champion. No cheerleading for me. Wrestling in the Everglades was my jam."

"Funny." He started the engine and as the car started, the radio also came on. An old Garth Brooks country song come on.

I looked over at him in surprise. "You listen to country music?"

"That surprises you?"

"Yes." I studied his classically handsome features and attire and laughed. "I mean, you went to boarding schools in England, and your mother lives in France and is a model."

"But my dad loved country music. His favorite musician was actually Hank Williams, Sr."

"No kidding?"

"Yeah, his favorite song was 'I'm So Lonesome, I Could Cry.' Do you know it?"

"No. It sounds sad, though."

"Yeah. It's about a man who's lost the will to live." He nodded. "It's a bit depressing. He played it a lot before he left."

"Aw, do you think it was his loneliness that killed him?"

"Hmm? Killed who? Hank Williams? He was 29 when he died, did you know? He had a heart attack in the back of his Cadillac. So sad."

"I was talking about your dad." I paused. "Though that's super sad about Hank Williams, I never knew that."

He frowned at the road ahead. "Let's change the subject. So, were you a cheerleader, then?"

"No, I told you I wrestled gators."

"And when you didn't wrestle gators?"

"When I didn't wrestle gators, I was on the swim team and the tennis team."

"So you *can* swim." He shook his head as he pulled out of the driveway. "And you can definitely race with me."

"Maybe. I wouldn't want to embarrass you, though." I pretended to do the breaststroke. "I went to Nationals twice. In fact, my coach said if I were to dedicate myself, I might have a shot at making the Olympics."

"But you didn't want to?"

I shook my head. "It would have meant disrupting my whole family. And I didn't want it enough. Plus, I was always more interested in going to college and writing."

"Your poetry?"

"Yeah." I nodded. "And I wanted to have a boyfriend," I admitted. "My parents never really let me date much, and I didn't have much time between studying and practice."

"So you wanted to go to college so you could have a life?"

"Something like that."

"And how was Columbia? It must have been quite a change of scene going from Florida to the big city."

"I had a mini panic attack when I arrived at LaGuardia and took a cab to my dorm that first year. It all seemed so big, so dirty, and so overwhelming. I wanted to cry and fly back home."

"But you didn't."

"I arrived on campus and fell in love." I smiled. "It was what I'd always imagined it would be like, and I finally felt at home. I was a small-town girl, but I always dreamed of living in the city."

"I can see that." He nodded.

"So, what about you? Why do you live in this small town?" I asked him, curiosity getting the best of me. "You're almost like a recluse. Do you just enjoy being away from people?"

"Do I just enjoy being away from people?" He glanced at me as he turned onto a dirt road. "Not really, no."

"So why?"

"Obligation."

"What obligation?"

"Nothing." He looked annoyed, and I wondered if I'd said something wrong. I didn't like it when Wade was grumpy and moody. I liked it when he was playful and teasing. And I liked it a lot when he was sexy and charming.

"So, where are we going?" I asked him, hoping to lighten the mood again. "Don't tell me we're going to town to do more shopping so that I can make more delicious dinners?"

"Funny." He laughed and swung the car to the right. We were now travelling along a mud road through the forest, and the truck was bumping up and down uncomfortably. "It's a surprise. You'll see."

"Is this truck going to make it? Is it a four-wheel drive?" I clutched the side of the car.

"Are you nervous? Don't worry, Savannah. You're in good hands."

"I daresay that I am."

"I daresay that you are." His voice was warm, and I sank back into the seat with a smile on my face and listened to the music coming from the speakers. The sound of a twanging guitar had me nodding my head to the beat. It wasn't a song that I knew, but I found myself humming along and enjoying it.

"This is so cool. Who is this? Is this Hank Williams, as well?"

"No, this is Scrapper Blackwell." He spoke in a twang. "'Nobody Knows You When You're Down and Out.'"

"Sorry, what?"

"That's the name of the song." He grinned. "Hold on, it's going to get bumpy."

"*Get* bumpy?" I laughed. "It's already bumpy." I gripped the side of the door even harder and stared ahead. The woods were getting denser, and there was less sunlight shining in through the windows. "Where are you taking me?"

"On an adventure. Welcome to Herne Hill Forest." He made a sharp left, and I slid towards him. "You okay?" He flung me a quick glance.

I gripped the door a little tighter and pulled myself back up. "I'm okay, thanks."

"Okay, five more minutes."

I looked at him in surprise. We were in the middle of nowhere. What were we going to do? Bird watch or climb trees? I giggled to myself at the thought of climbing trees. That would really be something, wouldn't it?

"Why are you giggling?" Wade looked over at me, an amused expression on his face.

"I was just picturing us climbing the trees, trying to crawl along branches to birdwatch."

"You really have an overactive imagination, don't you?"

"I have an imagination, yes." I shrugged. "Do you have a problem with that?"

"Never." He suddenly slammed on the brakes. "We're here."

"We're here?" I looked out of the windows. "Uhm, where?"

We were in the middle of the forest and I could see nothing but brush and trees.

"Yup." He opened his car door and walked and slammed his car down and walked to the back of the truck. He jumped into the back cab and began rummaging through some bags. I undid my seatbelt and got out of the truck.

"What are we doing?" I walked to the back, and he handed me a pair of sand brown hiking boots. "What are these for?"

"We're going on a hike."

"We are?" I took the boots and turned them over, surprised to see they were in my size. Wade then handed me a pair of wooly socks.

"Put these on. The boots are new and not broken in, but we're not going on a long hike, so it should be okay."

"You bought these for me?"

"Yup."

"When?"

"When I was in town the other day."

"You never told me."

"Surprise." He grinned and jumped off of the truck. "Now put them on."

"I'm so curious to find out where we're going."

"You'll find out soon enough."

"You're full of surprises, aren't you, Wade?"

"Yes," He smirked. "Though not all of my surprises are good."

"What does that mean?" I pulled my sandals off and slipped on the socks.

"Nothing for you to worry about." He watched me putting on the boots and then I double knotted the laces to make sure they didn't come undone. "You don't mind hiking, right?"

"As long as it's not too far." I looked up at him. "I'm not in the best shape."

"You look like you're in good shape to me."

"Looks can be deceiving."

A light seemed to shine in his eyes at my words. "How very true," he agreed. "Okay, ready?"

"I guess so. Are you going to tell me where we're hiking to? Should I bring my purse?"

"No, don't worry about it. No one will bother our stuff." He grabbed a bright yellow bag out of the back seat. I looked at it curiously, but he just smiled. "Come this way." He grabbed my hand and led me to a small clearing to the left of the truck. I was surprised that he had taken my hand, but I enjoyed the feel of his warm skin on mine.

"So, this a date, huh?" I asked, summoning up the nerve to ask him what was in my mind.

"Yes," he grinned as he looked down at me. "You said you wanted me to take you on a date."

"Well, actually, I said I'm not going to sleep with you when I haven't even been on a date with you." I licked my lips. "Is this all so you can sleep with me?"

"I don't know if I should answer that." He laughed and then he let go of my hand. He walked ahead of me and pulled some branches to the side. "Walk through, I'll keep them to the side." I slipped past the branches and then waited for him. I looked down to the ground where several slugs and snails were making their way along the ground. The trees provided shade from the sun, and as we continued walking, I could hear the sound of water.

"Are we going to a creek or something?" I asked him with a small smile. "Are we going swimming?"

"Something like that." He walked past me.

"So, what happened to your last assistant? I assume you had one, right?"

"I had one." His voice was lower now. "She's gone."

"Where did she go? Why did she leave?"

"Things became complicated ..." He stopped suddenly and looked at me. "Why are you asking?"

"I was just curious. I—"

I was interrupted by several loud cracks, the sound of branches breaking to the left of us. My gaze darted toward the noise, but I could see nothing there. No other humans and no animals. My eyes flew back to Wade and his danger-ously handsome face. I swallowed hard. Where the hell was this man taking me? And why did I feel like I would follow him to the ends of the earth, no questions asked?

"Let's continue with our walk and talk at the same time?" He started walking again, and I followed on his heels.

"Was she pretty?"

"Was who pretty?"

"Your last assistant."

"Where is this coming from?" He frowned. "Are you going to recite any of your poetry to me?"

"Maybe one day."

"Why not now?"

"I don't know."

"Please? He looked hopeful. "I'd love to hear one of your poems."

"I guess, but you have to promise not to laugh."

"I promise." He crossed his fingers and touched them to his heart. "I won't laugh."

"Fine, let me think." My heart was racing, but I was happy that he was paying an interest. I only hoped he liked them. "Okay, I have one that is fitting for today."

"Oh, yeah? I can't wait to hear it."

"Tall crashing waves, thunderous roars, grey skies, the way I feel when you're not here, timid, scared, uneasy. Sunshine, rainbows, a deer on the grass, the way I feel when you're near me. The forest dew tells a story, the owl in the trees sees it all, my heart, my soul, live in the sky, waiting on never, waiting on forever, waiting on sometimes. A white butterfly flutters by, stops on a petal, seeks a new beginning, makes me blink, makes me sing, makes me believe. A wolf stalks through the grass, smelling rather than seeing, trusting rather than knowing, and I just wait. Tall crashing waves, thunderous roars, uncertainty. All I can do is wait. And then maybe you'll come back to me." I stopped, cleared my throat and blushed as Wade just stared at me. "I'm done."

"He really broke your heart, huh?" His voice was full of sympathy.

"Who?"

"Whoever you wrote that poem for." He grabbed my hand and pulled me into his arms and stared into my eyes. "He wasn't worth it."

"I ..." My voice trailed off at the look in his eyes.

"If you ever write a poem for me, I would want it to be happy. I would want it to be full of joy."

"No one broke my heart." And it was true. No one had broken my heart. But that was the problem. I'd never really been in love. I craved a relationship that was worth writing poetry for. And as I stared at Wade, I knew that he was worthy of my poetry. Only I wasn't sure that I could promise that it would be happy.

"Good." He leaned down and kissed me tenderly, his fingers in my hair as he held me close to him. I could feel his heart beating against mine, and I kissed him back, loving the smell of him as I kissed him back. "You're a talented poet, Savannah." He stroked my hair. "Thank you for sharing that with me."

"You're welcome." I stared up at him, dazed with longing. If he was to attempt to take my clothes off right now, I would let him. If he wanted to strip me and make love to me right here, right now in the middle of the forest, I would let him. I didn't care about the bugs, I didn't care about the mud and leaves. I didn't care about anything. At this moment, there were only the two of us. I felt like we were Adam and Eve in the Garden of Eden, the only two people in the world. Just me and him. Wade and Savannah.

"Come on, let's keep going. I think we just have a mile more to go." He broke the stare and ran his hands through his hair. "I can't wait for you to see this."

"See what?" I bit back my disappointment as the moment between us vanished like smoke. I wanted to make love to him. I wanted to give myself to him. I wanted it to be a moment I'd remember for the rest of my life.

"You'll see." He laughed, looking happier. "I miss these moments," he said quietly, almost to himself. "Just being one with nature, not having to worry about everything in the world. Just taking each moment as it comes. Just believing in goodness." He snuck a look at me. "Sometimes when I'm with you, I feel like there is good in this world after all."

"Thank you." His words made my heart swell. "So, do you have any hidden talents that I don't know about?"

"Hmm, let me think …" He continued walking and a comfortable silence fell between us as we continued walking. "I guess I have the ability to make do in any situation."

"Oh? What does that mean?"

"I think that no matter what life throws my way, I figure out a way of keeping going." He nodded to himself. "Do you know that Nelson Mandela quote?"

"Which one?" And then I laughed. "I don't know why I said which one, I don't know any of his quotes."

"He said, 'The greatest glory in living lies not in never falling, but in rising every time we fall.'" He nodded to himself. "And that's what I do. No matter what happens, I continue rising."

"What do you rise from?" I asked softly.

He stopped then and smiled wistfully. "I wish I could tell you, Savannah Carter." He looked sad for a few seconds and then grabbed my hand. "We're nearly there." Excitement lit his face. "Come on, I'll race you."

He started running, and I ran after him, wondering what his secrets were and if I would ever find them out. I didn't catch him and was out of breath by the time he stopped, but when I finally caught up with him, I looked around me in awe. We were standing next to a small waterfall. The gushing water, the green trees, the birds flying by—it all looked like something from a movie. This amazing place had been well worth the short hike.

"Thanks for bringing me here, this is beautiful."

"Oh, this is just the beginning."

"Just the beginning?" I frowned. "We're going to keep hiking?"

"No, we're going swimming."

"Oh? Where?"

"We're going to jump."

"Jump?" My mouth dropped. "Jump where?"

He pointed down at the small lagoon beneath the water-fall. "We're going to jump from this waterfall into the water below."

"Oh, hell no!" I laughed. "There's no way. I do *not* want to die today."

"You won't die." He grinned. "We'll jump together. Take your boots and clothes off. I'll put them in my water bag."

"Are you being serious?" I swallowed hard and watched as he took off his clothes and boots and stuffed them in his bag. He was standing there in a pair of black swim trunks and a huge grin on his face.

"Yes."

"I can't do this."

"Do you trust me?" he whispered.

As I took in his dark eyes, with just a hint of playfulness in them, I knew that I did. I nodded slightly.

He grinned. "Take your clothes off."

I hesitated just a few seconds before I took off my boots and socks and handed them to him to put in the bag. Then I pulled off my top and shorts and handed those to him as well.

I stood there in my hot pink bikini. He nodded approvingly as he took in my appearance.

"I like it." He stepped closer to me and looked me up and down. "Very sexy."

"I wasn't going for sexy."

"Then it's just natural." He laughed boyishly as he put the rest of my clothes into his bag, clicked it shut, and put it on his back. "Come on, let's do this. I promise you will love it."

"You shouldn't make promises you can't keep."

"I don't." He grinned. "Follow me."

He walked around the side of the waterfall to a spot that seemed to be right in the center of the top of the waterfall. He looked behind and waited for me to catch up and then he pointed down. "You're aiming to hit that spot."

"There are rocks down there. We could crack our skulls open!"

"We won't." His voice was full of confidence. "Do you want to hold my hand and jump together?"

"No!" I laughed and shook my head. "No way!"

"Are you scared?"

"Yes, of course I'm scared!" My stomach was a ball of nerves and I could feel my legs trembling. "That's a long jump. How deep is the water?"

"It's a good 30-50 feet. You'll be okay."

"I don't know." I chewed down on my lower lip.

"Trust me, Savannah." His green eyes searched mine. "Do you want to watch me first?"

"Yes."

"Fine."

He took a few steps back then ran straight off the cliff, doing a backflip before straightening his body and slicing into the water. I held my breath for what felt like minutes, then gasped with relief when his head broke the surface.

"The water feels amazing!" he shouted up to me. "Absolutely amazing!"

"I bet it's freezing!"

"I wouldn't say freezing." He laughed as he swam around. "You can do it, Savannah!"

"I'm not sure." I looked down and my head started spinning. "It's so far!"

"But I'm here waiting for you at the bottom." He smiled up at me. "You can do it."

"Okay." I took a few steps back. "You can do this, Savannah," I whispered to myself and then took a deep breath and ran. I jumped and screamed as my arms and legs flailed through the air. I wanted to throw up, but before I had a chance to think about it, I was in the water. As I swam to the surface, I could feel the vibration of the water from the falls hitting the surface of the river. I took a deep gulp of air as my head met the cool air.

"You made it." Wade grinned as he swam over to me.

"I did." I started laughing. "I can't believe I did that!"

"I'm so glad you did." Treading water, he pulled me into my arms. "You looked so sexy jumping."

"No, I didn't." I put my arms around his neck. "I bet I looked like a scared rat."

"Not at all." He kissed me on the lips. "Did you enjoy it?"

"I was scared stiff," I admitted with a laugh as I ran my fingers through his hair.

"That's not the only thing that's stiff." I slapped him lightly on the shoulder. "You know what also feels amazing?"

"What?"

"Skinny dipping."

"Anything to get me out of my clothes, huh?"

"I've seen you naked before."

"And I've seen you naked before as well."

"Yes, you have." He grinned as his hand squeezed my ass. "You've even touched me naked. Taken me into your mouth naked." He winked.

"You're a fool." I ran my hands down his back and then pushed away from him and swam towards the land.

"Savannah?" he called after me and I could hear him swimming behind me. I quickened my pace and scrambled onto dry land. "Where are you going?"

I stood there and smiled at him, hoping I looked sexy. "Nowhere." I grinned and undid the top of my bikini, letting the flimsy material fall to the ground. My nipples tightened in the cool air, and I shivered slightly, but then when I saw the look of lust on Wade's face, I warmed up again quickly. Then I took a deep breath and took my bottoms off. I stood there naked and self-conscious, but then I heard Wade's sharp intake of breath. He got out of the water, dumped his bag on the ground, and pulled his trunks off.

I stared down at his cock and tried not to lick my lips. He was magnificent. I had to repress the urge to push him down to the ground and jump on top of him.

"You're beautiful." He walked over to me, his eyes on my breasts. "I can't lie, I want you so badly right now." He kissed my cheek and then trailed his mouth down my neck and along my collarbone.

"Do you?" I ran my fingers down his chest. His skin felt

J. S. COOPER

warm and silky. I moaned as he slipped a hand to my breast and gently stroked my nipple.

"I've never wanted anyone more than I want you in this moment." His eyes pierced into my heart. "I want to bend you over and fuck you so hard. I want you to scream my name so loud that every bird in the woods knows that I'm inside of you."

"Oh, Wade …" I felt wet just thinking about him inside of me. And then, because I didn't know what I wanted to happen, I ran back into the water and dived in. I swam for as long as I could without breathing and then came up for water. Wade was a few yards behind me.

"Follow me." He nodded towards the waterfall and we swam over to the side where it was shallow enough to stand. He stopped and faced me. "Close your eyes and lean your head back."

"Why?"

"Just do it."

"Okay." I nodded, closed my eyes and leaned my head back as I tread water. I could feel the lightest flicker of water droplets on my face. And then I felt the warm glow of the sun warming up my body. Suddenly Wade was behind me and holding my back.

"Just relax," he whispered into my ear, his hands massaging my shoulders. The pressure of his fingers kneading my muscles and the touch of his skin on mine felt amazing. I'd never felt such bliss.

"Don't stop," I whispered as he shifted behind me and he chuckled.

"Welcome to Utopia," he whispered back and started humming a song I'd never heard before. This was yet another perfect moment in our day. Wade Hart was making me feel things I'd never even imagined feeling. So many poems were bursting to be written and to be said. And the best part of it all was that I truly believed in my heart that Wade was falling for me as well. As I floated in the water, the sun kissing my face as his fingers massaged away my stress, I knew that tonight was going to be the night.

I was going to make love to the man I was falling in love with, and it was going to be the best night of my life.

CHAPTER 17

"How are you feeling?" Wade squeezed my knee as we pulled back up to the manor. I smiled at him lazily, my eyes half closed as I drifted between sleep and alertness, my entire body soaked in euphoria.

"Amazing. Absolutely amazing." I smiled at him. "I think this has been the most perfect day in my whole life."

"Well, I'm glad I got to experience it with you." He put the car in park and then turned to me. "You don't have to cook dinner tonight. I can order a pizza if you want."

"That sounds great."

"I guess you want to shower now?" He opened his door and got out and I got out as well.

"Yes, I think I would like that." I walked to the back of the truck to help him carry some of the bags.

"A nice shower and change of clothes will warm you right up."

"I don't think I want to change into any clothes," I said mischievously, peering up at him through my lashes.

"You don't?"

"I think I'd like to stay naked." I moved closer to him. "With you."

"With me?" He arched an eyebrow at me. "Are you sure?"

"I've never been more sure about anything in my life." I kissed his cheek and tugged on his shirt so that he would face me. "I want this, Wade."

"I want you as well," he growled and pulled me into his arms, kissing me roughly as he tugged on my hair. "Are you positive?"

"I'm positive." I kissed him back passionately, running my hands up under his shirt and touching his bare skin. "Let's go to your room."

"What about the shower?"

"We can shower together." I grinned.

He growled again, his teeth tugging on my lower lip as he squeezed my ass. "Let's go inside. I'll get this stuff later."

He tugged on my hand and we ran into the house, giggling like kids as we hurried to his bedroom. I noticed his mother in the kitchen as we ran down the corridor and I saw her frowning, but I ignored her. As we entered his room, Wade swept me up into his arms and carried me into the bathroom where he put me down and began taking off his clothes. I pulled my clothes off as well, and he pulled me into his arms and kissed me, my breasts crushed against his chest as his fingers tangled in my hair. Lust bloomed deep within me as I felt his erection hardening against my belly.

"Your moans alone are enough to make me come," he growled as he bent down and took a nipple into his mouth. He nibbled lightly on my most sensitive of spots then tugged slightly. I cried out at the slight flash of pain that heightened the intense pleasure. My fingernails ran down his back and around to his stomach, then he stilled as my hands went further down and I wrapped my fingers around his rigid cock. I moved my hand back and forth, relishing his groans of pleasure. I grinned at the moisture I felt on him and his cock grew even harder.

"*Fuck*." He pushed me back against the wall. The towel rack pressed into my back as his lips traced my neck. His right hand slipped between my legs and his fingers quickly found my clit and rubbed urgently. I moaned and closed my eyes at the exquisite pleasure that was building up. "You're so wet already." His teeth sank into my skin, and he slipped a finger inside of me. My legs buckled as he fingered me, while his thumb rubbed my clit. "I want to make you come a million times tonight," he grunted as I whimpered. "Fuck the shower, we're going to the bedroom." He picked me up as if I weighed nothing and he carried me back to bedroom.

Before I knew it, he was beside me on the bed, kissing me on the lips, his fingers playing with my breasts. He moved on top of me, and I spread my legs, eager to feel him inside of me. I looked up at him, towering over me, his green eyes dark and frenzied. He positioned himself at my entrance and rubbed the tip of his cock against my clit as I moved back and forth on the bed. His fingers found my nipple and he rubbed it gently before squeezing it a little more tightly. I cried out at the sensation, and he grinned down at me.

"So, you like a little pain with your pleasure, do you?" I shook my head as he kissed me hard. "I think you do." He chuckled as he bit down on my lower lip. "But we'll have to see."

"What do you mean?" I glanced up at him a little nervously.

"Not tonight." He grinned. "But later." His grabbed the side of my face. "Tonight, I will fuck you and give you all the pleasure you ever thought possible. Next time, I will fuck you and teach you things you never even imagined could feel good."

"Oh," I said breathlessly and pulled him down onto me. "Take me now, Wade. I want to feel you inside of me."

He groaned at my words and touched the side of my face lightly. "I wish you were on the pill." He rolled over and grabbed a packet from his side table. He ripped it open and took out a condom, which he slid easily onto his cock, as if he'd had lots of practice. I tried to ignore that fact that he probably had.

I gasped as he moved back on top of me, his hand guiding his cock to my opening. I moaned as he slipped a finger inside of me and rubbed my juices against my clit. I grabbed his back and then I felt the tip of him sliding into me. It felt uncomfortably tight, and I whimpered slightly.

"Open your legs wider." His hand reached down to spread my legs, and I stretched them out further. He inched his cock into me and after a few seconds he frowned. "Has it been a while since you had sex?" He kissed the side of my lips, and I nodded.

"Okay, I'll try to go a bit slower." He groaned as he inched himself into me further. I arched my back, and his cock went even further. I cried out in pain. His eyes widened, and he stopped. "Savannah?" He pulled out of me.

"What are you doing?" I groaned.

His expression had grown deadly serious. "Are you a virgin?"

"Yes," I said softly. "And I want you to fuck me now, please, sir."

He groaned at my words and I felt his body shuddering on top of me. "Fuck it, Savannah, but I can't say no."

"Then take me," I pleaded with him and sighed in pleasure as I felt the tip of him entering me again.

"It's going to hurt a little bit, but I promise you it will start to feel better."

"Okay." I nodded and I held him close to me. He kissed

me softly as he entered me and then I felt his cock push past something that caused me immediate pain. I blanched, and he paused. "Don't stop." I begged him, and he continued. He thrust into me a little harder, and I felt like he was filling me up completely.

"Oh, Savannah, you're so tight. I don't know how long I can last." He groaned and moved back and forth, his cock sliding in and out of me as my breasts bounced against his chest. I closed my eyes, and all of sudden the tight feeling didn't feel so bad. The pain morphed into pleasure, and as he thrust into me, the pleasure started to build.

"Oh, Wade, it feels good now!" I cried out. "Don't stop!" I squeezed my legs together.

Wade swore under his breath. "Say my name again, Savannah." His voice was raspy as he moved back and forth.

"Wade, don't stop!" I gasped as he increased his pace. His cock slid in and out of me and then I felt his fingers rubbing my clit at the same time. "Oh, my God!" I cried out as I felt the pleasure building up, wanting to explode. "Oh, Wade, oh, I think I'm going to come!"

"Come for me, Savannah. Come for me because I'm about to blow my load," he grunted, his cock slamming in and out of me.

"Oh, Wade!" I screamed as my body shuddered against him. His fingers kept rubbing my clit as he moved faster and faster. As I orgasmed, I grabbed his shoulders and kissed him hard. Suddenly he pulled out of me and flipped me onto my stomach. He pulled my shoulders up and my ass out until I was on all fours and then he entered me again and slammed into me from behind. I fell forward onto the bed as I cried out. It felt like he was entering me even deeper now, and as he grabbed my hips and slammed into me harder, a new wave of pleasure soared through me. He thrust faster and faster and then shuddered and slammed into me one last time. He groaned as he came and then he pulled out of me and rolled me back onto my back, kissing me on the lips. He pulled the condom off and placed it on the side table before pulling me into his arms.

"I want to make love to you again right now, but I don't want to make you too sore tomorrow." He stroked my cheek. "How are you feeling?"

"Amazing." I smiled at him. "Absolutely amazing. I want to do it again."

"Why don't we shower first and then see how you feel." He grinned. "I was a little rougher than I wanted to be just now, and I'm afraid if we go again, I'll be even rougher. Your body feels amazing." His fingers played with my nipples. "I want all of you. I want you again right now." He kissed my lips. "You're beautiful, Savannah."

"Thank you." I sighed happily and lay in his arms, feeling happier and more satisfied than I'd ever felt in my life.

◆◆◆

"I think the pizza I called for earlier is here. Do you want to go and grab the pizza from the front? I told them to leave it on the table," Wade asked as we walked back into the bedroom from the bathroom where we'd just showered together.

"Only if you promise to make love to me one more time."

"Are you sure? I want you to be able to walk tomorrow."

"I think I'll be okay." I grinned back and him, and he swatted me on the ass.

"That's what you think." He pulled me back into his arms and kissed me again. "I should fuck you hard and teach you a lesson."

"Teach me a lesson, huh?" I winked at him. "What lesson?"

"You'll see." He laughed. "Go and get that pizza, and I'll tidy up the bed." He nodded to the messy bed and we both laughed. "Also need to get rid of the used condom. Don't need that hanging around." He walked over to the side table and held it up. "You see how much I blew." I nodded shyly, and he laughed.

"I'm going to pull out next time." He threw the used condom in the trash can. "I'm going to pull out and come on your stomach." He walked back over to me and touched my stomach. "Is that okay?"

"I don't mind." I rubbed his bare chest. "If you want to."

"You'll feel how hot you make me." He grabbed my fingers. "And coming on your stomach is the next best thing to coming inside of you."

"You could come inside my mouth," I suggested.

His eyes widened. "Are you sure?"

"Yes." I nodded. "I wanted to feel and taste every part of you."

"I could go down on you right now." He licked his lips. "Go and get the pizza before I bend you over and fuck you right now."

"I don't mind."

"I can't have you collapsing from hunger, though." He pushed me away. "Now go and get the food."

"Okay." I batted my eyelashes at him over my shoulder before heading for the kitchen in a robe. I was thankful that his mother wasn't there, and I grabbed the box off of the table. As I picked it up, a piece of paper fell to the ground and I bent down to pick it up and scanned it quickly. It was a note:

. . .

"Dearest Savannah,

You think you know, but you don't. You think you're special, but you're not. You're not the first woman he's taken to the forest, and you won't be the last. There are many bodies buried there that you'll never know about. I advise you to leave my son alone and leave Herne Hill now. You're not good enough for him. And you will never be."

I stared at the note and then ripped it up, letting the pieces of paper fall to the ground. I was not going to let her come between me and Wade. Wade and I had something special. I hurried back to the bedroom with the pizza and smiled at the sight of a naked Wade stretched out on the bed waiting for me.

"Come, my dear."

"I thought we were going to eat first?"

"I changed my mind." He waved me toward him. "We can eat after I take you again. Come here."

I hurried to the bed, placing the pizza box on the night-stand before I got on the bed next to him. He leaned over and took my dressing gown off, raking my naked body with his gaze. He pushed me back onto the bed and kissed the side of my neck. I looked down at the bed and noticed he'd changed the sheets.

"Did we dirty them?" I asked him self-consciously.

"Only with a bit of blood." He winked. "It will wash out."

"Are you sure?"

"Oh, yes."

He kissed down my stomach until his lips were between my legs. I moaned as the tip of his tongue grazed my clit and he started licking me back and forth. His tongue slid into me, and I allowed myself to be carried away with pleasure. I came on his face and then he reached to grab for another condom and entered me again. This time he was rougher and faster, and I felt like every part of me was going to explode. I came quickly, and he grunted as he slammed into me a few times and then pulled out. He rolled his condom off and then I felt him spurting his cum all over my breasts.

His eyes glazed over as he took in the sight. "You're so beautiful lying there in my cum," he groaned as he dropped down and kissed me on the cheek. "I think we will need to shower again."

"I think you might be right." I stroked his cheek. "I think I'm falling in love with you, Wade Hart."

He pulled away from me, his expression growing dark. "Oh, no, Savannah, you cannot fall for me. I'm not the guy you fall for."

"But Wade ..." I protested, but he pushed his fingers against my lips.

"Shh. That's enough." He kissed me and his eyes darkened. I felt his fingers rubbing my clit and I writhed on the bed, growing wet all over again.

"But Wade ..."

"But nothing." He moved his fingers away and then pushed them between my lips. "Taste yourself on my fingers, Savannah. See how sweet you taste? How sweet you are? I can only ruin you." He rolled me on top of him, my pussy rubbing back and forth on his cock. "I could slip inside of you right now." His eyes hooded as he gazed up at me. "I could have you riding me bareback and think nothing of it." I moaned as he held my hips in place. "I could ruin you, Savannah. I could absolutely ruin you."

"Maybe I want you to," I said softly

He pulled me off him and rolled away, his expression

oddly blank. "Go and shower. I need to make a call." He jumped off of the bed. "Then we can eat."

I got off of the bed, wishing I hadn't ruined the moment by telling him I loved him, and crept into the bathroom to shower. I turned the water on and was about to get in when I realized I needed a clean towel. We'd gone through the dry ones the first time we'd showered and they were now wet. I opened the door to head back into the bedroom and stopped. Wade was on the phone, his back to me, and his voice was low and urgent.

"I've fucked up, Henry. I can never let her know the truth. This whole thing was a mistake. A huge mistake. I never should have created that ad. She can destroy everything. Absolutely everything. I never should have let Savannah Carter into our lives. If she learns the truth, we'll be ruined."

Thank you for reading To Whom It May Concern. Part two of the duet is Return To Sender and will be out in three weeks. Continue reading for an exclusive teaser.

.

Printed in Great Britain
by Amazon